Framed in Fire

Framed in Fire

David Patneaude

*

Albert Whitman & Company

Morton Grove, Illinois

Also by David Patneaude:
Someone Was Watching
The Last Man's Reward
Dark Starry Morning: Stories of This World and Beyond
Haunting at Home Plate

Library of Congress Cataloging-in-Publication Data

Patneaude, David.
Framed in fire / by David Patneaude.
p. cm
Summary: When his stepfather conspires to keep thirteen-year-old Peter at a
mental institution, Peter begins to piece together secrets about his past with
the help of his younger brother's strangely prophetic dreams.
ISBN 0-8075-9098-3 (hardcover)
ISBN 0-8075-9096-7 (paperback)
[1. Stepfathers—Fiction. 2. Fathers and sons—Fiction.
3. Psychiatric hospitals—Fiction.] I. Title.
PZ7.P2734Fr 1999
[Fic]—dc21
98-39606
CIP
AC

10 9 8 7 6 5

The design is by Scott Piehl.

To every kid who hears a different drum.
And listens. And to grownups who
take the time to understand.

Many thanks to Natalie Roman, who, when this
story was just sparks and tinder, gave me her time
and provided her insights about the inside.

One

Before Buck, before I knew the word *stepfather*, I thought of the pieces of my life as normal and normal-sized. But then my life was changed by a big man with big ideas and big cars. After Buck and my mom got married, there was a big house, a bigger family, a big baby brother named Lincoln.

I was at our neighbor's house when Buck called from the hospital. "A boy," Mrs. Demmert said to me, smiling, still on the phone. Then her eyebrows went up. "Twelve pounds, fifteen ounces!"

They brought Lincoln home. My mom seemed exhausted, but Buck looked proud—prouder even than on his TV commercials, where he pushed those big fancy cars and invited folks to come in and take a test drive at Buck Champagne Motors, Brown County's only Lincoln Mercury dealer.

The changes took a new direction: It was Lincoln this and Lincoln that, and oh, yeah, what's

new with you, Peter? Nothing was new with me, except that I felt myself fading, like a watercolor that's been thinned down so much it becomes transparent.

What kept me from vanishing altogether was a surprise: Lincoln. Before he was born, I'd decided not to like him, and for a couple of weeks afterward I succeeded. Until he smiled at me. Until he grasped my finger with his doughy little hand and squeezed. I found myself spending more and more time in his room, playing with him or just watching him sleep. By the time he could walk, he could say my name. "Petah," he would say as he followed me around the house like a sturdy shadow. Sometimes it almost seemed like he knew what I was going to do next.

As Lincoln got older, he became the real centerpiece of our household. I got older, too; I thought I was doing okay. Not everyone agreed.

I was ten or eleven years old when I heard Buck mention the word *hyperactive* for the first time. His friend Lowell, Buck told my mom, had a hyperactive kid. Buck went on and on about how the kid acted, the doctor he saw, the pills he took.

What's the point? I wondered. But then Buck took my breath away; he slipped my name into the conversation like it belonged there, like Lowell's kid and I were partners in crime.

The first surprise was that he'd brought up my name at all. What I'd come to expect from Buck was about what he gave our dog, Cowboy: food, shelter, a command now and then. The second stunner was that he felt so free to talk about me while I was right there, as if I really was just a dog. But the real shocker was hearing him try to convince my mom there was something wrong with my head.

She danced around the subject the first few times Buck brought it up. "Do you really think so?" she'd say, or "Interesting." And that would put him off for a while—months, sometimes. But I'd have some problems, and he'd bring up the topic again and again. Each time it emerged more powerful, harder to ignore.

My problems weren't a big mystery. I'd heard the complaints, I'd seen the worried looks, I'd carried home notes from my teachers. Over the years I'd been to the principal's office on several occasions—three times since I'd started seventh grade. I hadn't considered that any of that stuff meant I was hyperactive, whatever that was. I thought I was just being a kid. I didn't like labels; I didn't like the feel of Buck's words, the way my mom got defensive. What was he up to? Who could help me figure it out?

My buddy Dillon was a year older than me. A year smarter, I figured. I decided to ask him what he thought.

We were at his house, watching a Rangers game on TV. I wasn't really watching or listening. I was thinking about Buck and his mysterious campaign. "Buck's trying to mess with me," I blurted out.

Dillon hit the mute button and looked at me from the other end of the couch. "What do you mean?"

I told him about Buck's friend with the hyperactive kid, how Buck had the idea clenched between his teeth like a bulldog with a bone.

"Hyperactive?" Dillon said. "You?"

"Sometimes now Buck calls it something different: ADD, or ADHD. He thinks he's a doctor. So far my mom isn't convinced."

"I knew some kids at my old school that were hyperactive."

"How could you tell?" I said.

He shrugged. "Problems with their grades, or they'd be taking pills or seeing a counselor. Sometimes you just knew by the way they acted, or they'd be getting in trouble a lot."

"Like me?" I said. "You think Buck's right about me?"

He touched the off button on the remote. The screen went blank, and he studied me in the silence. I figured he was recalling my behavior over the two years he'd lived next door.

"I know you pretty good by now," he said finally.

"So?"

"So to me you're not hyperactive. To me you're pretty much regular."

"Pretty much regular?"

He smiled. "You're not always the easiest guy to get along with. Especially when Buck's involved."

"What do you think he's up to?" I said.

"Sounds like he wants your mom on his side."

"And then what?"

"I'd guess you'd be visiting a doctor."

"Could you just tell them I'm okay?" I said, but I knew the answer already.

"I'm a kid. They wouldn't care what I think."

"I don't want to go to a doctor."

"It wouldn't be so bad. The doctor's not going to make up something."

"Not so bad? Someone examining my life, trying to tell me how to live it?"

Dillon shrugged again. I could tell he didn't think this was such a big deal. "Play Buck's game then. Do what he says. Stay out of trouble."

"No problem. Just like that."

"You can do it if you want."

"How?"

He didn't have a quick answer, but by the end of the afternoon we'd come up with a plan.

For the next couple of months I did my best to follow it. Instead of playing video games and speed-surfing the TV channels when my mom and Buck were around, I'd play one-on-one with Dillon or shoot baskets alone or take a walk or read. I cleaned my room and hung up my clothes; I stayed at the dinner table till everyone was done. When I couldn't avoid Buck, I tried to be polite to him, even when he called me Petey. At school, I sat still in class and kept my mouth mostly shut. I did my classroom work; I did my homework; I wrote neater.

I stayed away from Blaine Corbett, who was the main reason I'd been in trouble at school. He and I were like oil and water. Our disagreements often grew into arguments, then shoving matches, then fist-flying, grappling, sweating, falling-down, bloody, clothes-trashing fights. It wasn't pretty. In fact, it was the ugliest, most in-your-face example of how far I needed to go to prove myself. I figured if I could put my problems with Blaine Corbett behind me, I'd be on my way.

Two

I thought things were going okay. That's why I was surprised one day when I overheard Buck bringing up his friend's kid again. He was worse; they were thinking about putting him in a hospital. I knew what kind.

"What's that got to do with us, Buck?" my mom asked, while I hovered outside their bedroom door. That was all the opening he needed. He told her I was still behaving like Lowell's kid: I didn't pay attention; I was having trouble in school; I was fighting for no reason; I couldn't sit still; I was disrespectful; I was mean to Lincoln; blah, blah, blah.

I expected my mom to stick up for me. What did Buck know? He was a car salesman, not a doctor. And she did, kind of. She told him she'd noticed a big improvement; how could he not?

"It won't last," Buck said. "Unless we get him some help—some professional help—his true nature will come back."

"That's not fair," my mom said after a long

pause. "Peter didn't have problems when he was younger."

"Before I came around, you mean?"

"That's not what I meant. But things did change for him, especially after Lincoln was born." Her voice sounded thick and unsteady.

"Lots of kids have younger brothers."

"Lincoln is much younger. A half-brother. Peter had me to himself for a long time."

"Those ain't excuses."

"They're explanations, Buck."

"*Your* explanations. I think we need an expert's opinion. It's not fair to Peter or the rest of this family for you to just stick your head in the sand."

I waited for my mom's response; it came as soft humming, musical, familiar. The argument was over. Buck's last words had been spit out in that ugly bully tone he used when he'd run out of patience. I hated it when he got that way.

I couldn't imagine my real dad being so stubborn. I knew there'd been a divorce before he died, but when I got my mom to talk about it at all, she blamed it on their being too young. She never said anything bad about my dad; she barely said anything at all about him. I only knew he'd drowned in a fishing accident.

My mom had given up the fight. Soon they were talking to my teacher, and the school counselor, and the principal. I started getting that Weird Kid treatment at school: different assignments, and double checking, and visits to the counselor, and special tests, and long stares from teachers. Dillon ignored it; he stuck with me. But the other kids noticed; they started to leave me out of things. I could feel their eyes on me whenever I was singled out for some of the lab-rat stuff.

I figured the exorcist would be next, but I guess Buck couldn't find one in the yellow pages. Instead, I got to go see Dr. Fiske. I'd been to him before for checkups and sore throats.

The two of us sat in one of his little rooms and just talked. We covered lots of things, but mostly stuff about me—school, my parents, Lincoln, my friends, what I liked to do. We spent most of the time talking about basketball. Finally, Dr. Fiske smiled, which I thought was a good sign, and shook hands with me. He asked me to wait while he went out and talked to my mom and Buck.

I think they didn't like what he told them; I think he told them there was nothing wrong with me. I didn't go back to see Dr. Fiske again.

On the advice of his buddy with the hyper kid, Buck handpicked the next guy. Dr. Lubber wasn't very old, but he had lots of degrees framed on his wall—a bunch more than Dr. Fiske had. He asked me a ton of questions, and every time I said anything, he'd move his little wire-rimmed glasses down to the end of his nose and stare at me like he was trying to look inside a damaged clock.

I sat up straight, answered his questions, acted myself. I counted his smiles—three, all phony. I gave him back twice as many, as real as I could get them. I was *co-op-er-at-ing*. But halfway through my answer to his question about why I hated Lincoln (I was trying to explain to him that I didn't), his snaky eyes, magnified by his glasses, got to me. I stopped, right in the middle of a sentence. I was tired. I was done.

He waited.

"I think your customers are lining up outside," I said.

"Patients."

"Whatever."

"You're done talking, Peter?"

"I think you have your mind made up. I don't think you understand kids. I don't think you even like them."

He smiled again. Four phony ones now. And as he did I realized I was right: he didn't understand me; he didn't like me. He was exactly what Buck had been looking for. "I care about my patients, just as your parents care about you."

"Parent."

It was the wrong thing to say: he scribbled something on his note pad. Then we stared at each other for a while before he got up and showed me to the door, wearing phony smile number five. I sat out in the waiting room while he talked with my mom and Buck. They weren't in there very long, and when they came out, my mom would barely look at me. Buck was smiling. I knew I was in trouble.

By the next day I was taking two kinds of pills and struggling with the idea that I'd been officially declared different.

A week later, I'd lost energy, lost my appetite,

lost my way. I felt like I'd been condemned without a trial. Desperate, I cornered my mom after school. She was in the backyard, stuffing a big wooden pot with yellow flowers while Lincoln played in the sandbox in the far corner of the yard.

"Can I talk to you, Mom?" I said.

She looked up and smiled a cautious smile. "What about, Peter?"

"Me."

Her eyes got suspicious, and at first I thought maybe she was going to tell me no. But what would she use for an excuse? She stood, then perched her rear on the edge of a nearby bench and patted the space next to her. "Okay," she said. I sat. She folded her arms and stared into my eyes. She waited, but I wasn't sure how to begin. A trickle of sweat ran down my back and pooled at the top of my shorts.

"Do you really think there's something wrong with me, Mom?" I said finally.

She shrugged, like Dillon had. Her eyes clouded over. "I don't know," she said.

"Who does, then?"

"Dr. Lubber, I guess. He's the expert."

"So you're just going to believe what he says?"

"What choice do I have?"

"Can't I go see some other doctors? If they all think I'm nuts, I'll go along with it. But maybe they won't."

"Dr. Lubber's supposed to be the best around here. And nobody thinks you're nuts, Peter."

"Then why do I have to take the pills? They're making me sick."

She put her hands together in her lap and twisted her fingers until her knuckles cracked. "There's nothing wrong with taking medicine. It can be helpful. It's helped me."

I'd seen her bottles of pills lined up like chessmen across the back of her bathroom countertop. Childproof caps and names five syllables long and no explanation for why. But now I had a clue. Maybe the way she acted sometimes—jumpy and timid—wasn't just from Buck throwing his weight around. Maybe she had a problem inside her head. Maybe I inherited mine from her.

"What if the pills don't work?" I said. "What if Buck and Lubber still aren't happy with the way I'm acting?"

"I'm sure they'll work. I can see a difference already."

She was lying. I could tell by the way her eyes drifted away from me.

"What if they don't? What if they want to lock me up in a place with rubber walls and one-way mirrors, like Lowell's kid?"

"How do you know about that?"

"Why can't we just leave? We could go off some-where—you, me, and Lincoln—and live on our own."

I expected her to look at me like I really was crazy, or send me to my room, but she didn't. She gazed off toward Lincoln, busy with his toy cars and noises, but her eyes weren't focusing on any-thing as close as the corner of our backyard. I waited, silent, for her to say something. Her hands were moving, trembling.

"Life's never perfect, Peter," she said finally, her voice soft and scratchy. "Even though when you're a kid you think it should be."

"I don't think it should be perfect. I just want it to be the way it was."

"It wouldn't be."

"We could try."

"Buck's not a monster, Peter. He's not Superman, but I knew that when I married him. He's given me no reason to want to leave. He's good to me, great with Lincoln."

"And with me?"

She got up and went back to the flower pot, stabbing the trowel into the soft dirt, stuffing flowers into the holes, slapping the soil firm around the roots. She began humming to herself. It was a song we'd sung in church: "Sweet Hour of Prayer." I stood to leave. I figured she wasn't going to answer me.

Finally she stopped humming and looked up. Her eyes were wet. "You think leaving's the answer, Peter? It's not. We'd have nothing."

"We'd have each other."

"That's not enough. You have to give Buck a chance. If you don't, your worst nightmare could come true."

She turned her back on me and speared at the dirt, slicing a stem in half. The flower fell to the ground between her knees. She picked it up with shaking hands and tried sticking it back in the soil. It flopped over. She ignored it; she ignored me. She dropped her hands and sat back on her heels and let her chin sink down to her chest. Her shoulders began jerking up and down; I knew she was crying. I thought maybe I should give her a hug, but it didn't seem right. This was *my* problem; I should be getting the hug. Why was *she* getting so upset?

I walked away, toward Lincoln, trying not to think about my worst nightmare. It was daytime; the sun was out; Lincoln was building a sand city for his little cars, putting the finishing touches on a new building. On top of it a rose-petal flag flew from a twig flagpole. Outside a red aid car and a white ambulance were parked. Lincoln looked up at me and smiled. "Will you play cars with me, Peter?" *Peter*, now. No more *Petah*.

I sat on the corner bricks and put my hand over his. He backed the ambulance out of the hospital parking lot and started making siren sounds. Heat rose from the little city and hung in the air around me, but I shivered.

Three

I tried to do even better, to be smarter and happier and calmer. To be more like Lincoln. But my mom and Buck didn't seem to notice the difference. They kept me going to Dr. Lubber once a week. He kept me on the pills, my little tickets to the land of Nod.

Things got quiet for me for a while, mainly because my mom and Buck stopped paying much attention to me. They had something else to think about: Lincoln had become a TV star.

Buck got the idea while watching some little kid in a hamburger commercial. Next thing I knew, Lincoln was dressing up Buck's lame TV spots. They featured Lincoln standing on the hood of a car chosen as the Jumbo Deal of the Week. Buck would throw a football and Lincoln, dressed in a football uniform, would launch himself from the hood, catch the ball in mid-air, spike it through an open car window, land on his feet, and do a victory dance.

Most of it was just tricky camera work and special effects, of course. But one part of the commercial was definitely true: Lincoln could flat out catch a football.

Lincoln was a celebrity, attracting attention everywhere. As for me, I'd never felt more invisible. And I kind of backslid a little.

I opened the newspaper one day and found an article on Buck's commercials. What kind of father would exploit his little child like that? the reporter wondered. A boycott of the dealership would be a proper response, the article concluded.

I folded the paper just right and left it where Buck would be sure to find it.

He yelled at my mom about me, he called the paper, he threatened to sue, he spouted off about Lincoln getting a one-of-a-kind opportunity.

I survived Buck's anger—the cold looks, the silent treatment—and things continued on uneventfully for a while. Lincoln stayed in the spotlight; when I wasn't somewhere with Dillon, I was in my room, where nobody bothered me.

I'd sort through my sports cards or read or stare

at the ceiling. I'd think of my dad, wondering what he'd felt when he died, what it was like to drown. I wondered what my life would have been if he'd lived. I imagined him as some kind of spirit looking at me from far away. He couldn't help me; I knew it. But I hoped and prayed that somehow he would.

I'd almost made it through the school year without tangling with Blaine Corbett again. But on the next-to-last day of school he came looking for me outside, after lunch.

"Hey, Petey." He said it the way Buck did, only high-pitched, like chalk on a blackboard.

"I'm busy, Cor-butt."

"I saw your blimp of a brother on TV last night, Petey. Who's his tailor? Goodyear?"

I walked away, heading for the school.

"Lincoln's a good name for the little cruiser for now, but he'll be bigger than a car before long. Then you'll have to call him something else. How about Whale Boy?"

I could hear the repulsive rasp of his breathing as he followed me, giggling.

"Shut up, Cor-butt."

"I can picture him floating up on the beach with a harpoon stuck in his fat gut."

I turned and faced him up close. He stopped, his grin faded, he started to raise his hands. Too late. I swung hard and felt his flesh against my knuckles. His hands shot up to his nose, and I watched as blood oozed through his fingers. He dropped to his knees on the grass, staring at his hands. His voice—a high-pitched howl—rose like a siren in the hot Texas air.

A teacher grabbed me before I had time to admire my handiwork. The principal called my mom and Buck. Blaine's parents came, threatening to call a lawyer. Nobody wanted to hear my story.

I spent more time—most of the first two weeks of summer vacation—in my room. Not voluntarily. And it wasn't the same—now my room seemed more like a cell than a safe place. I tried to talk to my mom, but she wasn't impressed. A normal kid would've walked away, she said. A normal kid wouldn't have gotten into the other fights. We were lucky that Blaine's nose wasn't broken, that he didn't lose an eye, that we hadn't been sued.

After I came off restriction I kept a low profile, avoiding Buck whenever I could. And I sensed him avoiding me, too, as if he thought he could ignore me out of existence. I felt like a ruptured appendix waiting to be removed.

Then Lincoln fell down the stairs.

It was the Fourth of July and late, and Lincoln was asleep after a long night of watching fireworks. I was halfway up the stairs on my way to bed when I heard his door slam open.

"Fire!" he yelled.

He raced into view, hair sticking up, pajamas flapping, and hit the stairs. I froze. "Fire, Peter!" He was wide-eyed, flying, and just as he swerved around me, he tripped and fell. He bounced down the rest of the stairs head first and lay in a lump on the hardwood floor, still and silent.

Buck must have heard the commotion, because he and I got to Lincoln at the same time. I figured Buck's first concern would be Lincoln, but instead he grabbed me by the collar with one fist and punched me in the chest with the other. Not his hardest, maybe, but enough to knock the wind out of me and put my rear end on the stairs.

"You crazy jerk!" he shouted. He knelt down to look at Lincoln.

I was trying to catch my breath and talk at the same time. I couldn't do either. Tears blurred my eyes. "F-F-F—" I said.

Lincoln stirred and raised his head. "Fire!" he yelled. He tried getting to his feet.

Buck pushed past me and up the stairs when Lincoln let out a howl. "N-o-o-o-o-o! Not our house! The Demmerts'!"

The Demmerts. Our neighbors. Their little girl, Tracy Ann, was Lincoln's age. Lincoln loved Tracy Ann. He got up and staggered along the wall, heading for the front door.

I sucked in enough air to get to the phone on the hall table. I gave the 911 operator the Demmerts' address. Buck was trying to ask Lincoln how he knew about the fire, trying to tell me to hang up the phone, that it must've been a dream.

I didn't hang up. Lincoln's face told me no way. He was struggling with Buck, begging him to go to the Demmerts' house. My mom showed up just as the operator said, "They're on their way."

I dropped the phone and ran outside with Buck

and Lincoln on my tail. When I glanced back I saw my mom—wearing a wispy red robe—framed in the light from the doorway. For an instant she looked like *she* was on fire. But it was confusion that flickered in her eyes. As usual.

The Demmerts' front yard smelled of smoke. Buck must've smelled it, too. He left Lincoln at the edge of the yard and began pounding on the front door while I rang the doorbell. No answer. I took off around back.

There, the smoke smell was stronger. When I looked up at the rooftop, I saw the yellow-red lick of flame and the shadowy outline of black smoke against the sky.

"Fire!" I yelled. "Fire!"

I tried the French doors, but they were locked. I thought of the "universal key"—the axe—a fireman had once showed us at school. I didn't have an axe, but I quickly found a rock—a big one, softball-sized and heavy.

From six feet away I heaved it with all my might. Glass exploded. I reached through, unlocked the door, and pushed it open. I hung back, afraid to go in, and ten seconds later the

Demmerts' security alarm went off.

By the time I got back to the front yard, I could hear fire engines in the distance, and the Demmerts were staggering out the door. Mr. Demmert, dressed in his boxers and nothing else, had Tracy Ann in his arms. He was wheezing and coughing, but she was smiling. When Mr. Demmert set Tracy Ann down, Lincoln gave her a hug that wouldn't quit.

The firemen put out the fire, but the roof and the top floor were mostly destroyed. Fireworks were the cause, they said, landing on the roof, smoldering, then flaming up. And the smoke alarm was faulty. Eventually they figured out it was my setting off the burglar alarm that woke up the Demmerts and maybe saved their lives. Mr. Demmert took me and Dillon to dinner and a Rangers game and gave me a baseball autographed by Nolan Ryan. Mrs. Demmert bought me a book about real-life heroes and had the newspaper article about the fire and my role in it framed for my wall.

I think my mom was proud of me, although she didn't say much. The kids I knew treated me a little better, mostly. But Buck had nothing good to say. He figured what I'd done just proved once and for all that I was out of control. He said if I'd been thinking like a normal person, I would've ignored the advice of a little kid instead of dialing 911. I wouldn't have hurled a rock through a neighbor's window.

No one but me ever asked Lincoln about his dream. I think my mom and Buck were afraid to, and they didn't tell anyone else exactly what had brought us flying across the street in the middle of a hot summer night. When I asked Lincoln about it the next day, he told me he'd seen it in a "real" dream, as if he had at least a couple different kinds.

"I was in Tracy Ann's room, Peter. She was asleep, but I could hardly see her. I looked at the ceiling, and there were cracks lit up with fire. I yelled at Tracy Ann to wake up, but she wouldn't."

"And then what?"

"I ran fast. I ran for help. It was real."

I recalled another time a couple of years before when I'd gone into Lincoln's room at night and found him crying in his sleep. He couldn't tell me why. Scared, maybe, or too young to put it in words.

The next day we found our dog Cowboy stiff and cold in a ditch. A car had gotten the better of him sometime during the night. I never put the two things together until after the fire, until Lincoln told me about his real dream, and I started thinking he'd probably had those kinds of dreams before.

But I didn't spend a lot of time wondering about Lincoln or his dreams. I had my own problems. While everybody outside our family was thinking I was some kind of hero, Buck was saying I was some kind of loose cannon, that I was a danger to Lincoln.

"He did it on purpose," I heard him tell my mom one morning a few weeks after the fire. I was almost to the kitchen, and I didn't stop. They looked up from the table.

"You have someplace to be, Petey?"

"You guys talking about me?" I don't know why I asked. I knew the answer; their faces confirmed it. "What did I do on purpose?"

"You pushed Lincoln down the stairs. You tried to hurt him. Or worse."

I almost smiled. He had to be kidding. "Why would I do that?"

"You don't like him, Petey. Especially now that he's on the TV. You're jealous."

"Yeah. Like I want to be in one of your stupid commercials."

"People love those commercials."

"They'd love 'em more if you weren't in 'em."

Buck's face reddened. He glared at me, then at my mom.

"Peter's never done anything like this before, Buck," my mom said.

"It only *takes* one time," Buck growled. "We were lucky."

"What did I do?" I asked. "Lincoln tripped. I didn't push him. I can't believe you'd think I did," I said to my mom.

She shrugged and looked at Buck for support.

"Ask him," I said. "Ask Lincoln if I pushed him."

"We did ask him," my mom said. "He doesn't know. He just remembers his dream, and waking up at the bottom of the stairs."

I went to the kitchen door and shouted for Lincoln, who was watching TV in the family room. He came running, but slowed to a shuffle when he got to the door and looked at our faces.

"Lincoln," I said, crouching down to face him, "what made you fall down the stairs on the Fourth of July?"

He looked at Mom and at Buck, who was grinning like a salesman. He shrugged.

"Did I push you down the stairs, Lincoln?"

"You wouldn't push me, Peter."

"Did I?"

"He don't know, Petey." Buck's grin had disappeared.

"Is that right, Lincoln? You don't know?"

I said it too loud. Tears formed in his eyes. "I don't 'member, Peter." He reached out his hand and I took it. "I 'member you and Dad helping me up from the floor and my head hurting."

I stood. "He doesn't remember, so you guys just figure I pushed him? You're sick."

I let go of Lincoln's hand and walked over to my mom, who shrank away from me. Had Buck convinced her I could do something to hurt *her*?

"You're going along with him?" I asked her. She glanced toward Buck; her head twitched. I took it as a nod. "Sometimes I wish I would've been on that boat with my dad."

Buck started to get up from his chair. "That's enough of your mouth, Petey. When you're done with your breakfast, clear these dishes for your momma."

"Why wait?" I leaned over the table and swept the mess away with two quick swipes. Buck hotfooted it back, cursing, as dishes, cereal boxes, a milk carton, and assorted other stuff hit the floor. I turned and stomped away, heading for the solitude of my room. There was no point in sticking around.

✻

A week later my fate was sealed. I was in my room, waiting to leave for the hospital when I heard Lincoln's voice outside my door.

"Peter!"

I didn't answer. I wasn't in the mood. I was trying to keep myself from crying.

He knocked.

"Yeah?" I said.

He opened the door and came in. "I dreamed about the man with wings again, Peter."

I pretended to study the back of the book I was holding—*The Further Adventures of Hawk Ripley*—although I'd long before memorized every millimeter of its scratched and faded cover.

"It was in color and everything. You wanna hear about it, Peter?"

"I've heard about it."

"He talked this time. He might be coming to get you."

"What did he say?"

"Your name. He said 'Peter'."

"That's it, Lincoln? My name? He didn't tell you where I was going? How long I was going to be locked up?"

"Locked up? They're gonna lock you up? Mom said you were going to the hospital."

"Not a regular hospital. They're going to lock me in a rubber room and watch me through a fake mirror and take notes like I'm some kind of lab chimp."

"Why? Is it 'cause you're hyper? Dad says you're hyper."

"What's that mean?"

Lincoln stroked his chin just like Buck did when his brain was in gear. "Not sitting still in church?"

I remembered squirming a bit during a particularly boring sermon one time and Buck grabbing my ear and twisting till the whole side of my head burned. My mom looked straight ahead, pretending not to see. Lincoln stared wide-eyed until tears inched down my cheeks, and he looked away.

"I guess not sitting still might be an example," I said.

"The hospital will teach you to sit still?"

"Yeah."

"Then you can come back home?"

"I don't think they want me here, Lincoln."

He didn't say anything, but he looked like he was getting ready to cry. Five years old, but he knew I wasn't lying.

"Want to wrestle, Lincoln?" I didn't feel like it, but I thought maybe it would cheer up both of us. He gave me a smile and got down in a crouch, legs and arms spread, jaw set. I got on my knees, ready for the attack.

He came at me, legs churning, head down.

I caught him, rolled to my back, and let him scramble onto my stomach and chest, taking half the wind out of me. He reached for my arms, trying for a quick pin.

The door flew open. "I told you no more wrestlin' with him, Petey. You wanna get his face messed up?"

Petey. I hated that name.

"I thought I told you to knock," I said.

He glared at me like he was considering some kind of drastic action. "You're under some stress, so I'm gonna ignore your smart mouth, Petey."

"Okay, Bucky."

"Why don't you get off your skinny butt and haul it and your suitcase downstairs. Your momma's ready to go."

Lincoln started to cry.

Four

It was an hour's drive to Big Rock, home of Resthaven Hospital and not much else. I sat on the edge of the back seat and watched the empty flat miles hum by way too fast. We caught up with a cattle truck, and as Buck drew even with it, I saw a big brown eye staring through the bars. Eyeing me, eyeing the leather seat, the steer glimpsed its fate. I knew how that poor animal felt.

At least I had Lincoln. He sat close beside me, his hand in mine. I looked at my watch. A half-hour had passed already. "How long do I have to stay there, Mom?"

"That's up to the doctors and you, Petey," Buck said. My mom gave him a look but didn't say anything. As usual.

"If it was up to me I wouldn't be going at all."

"You couldn't prove it by your behavior," Buck said.

My behavior. I slumped back in the seat and thought of when my behavior had been just fine:

when it was me and my mom; before Buck; before Lincoln. Even Buck had been okay at first, taking me places and bringing me stuff. But that was then; this was now. This was what my mom had warned me about during our little backyard talk: my worst nightmare come true. I closed my eyes and held tight to Lincoln's hand.

✻

Resthaven Hospital wasn't what I'd pictured. What I'd imagined was something from another nightmare: story upon story of bricks and bars, surrounded by barbed wire and concrete; kids dressed in striped pajamas wandering the grounds like zombies, grim-faced guards on their heels.

The real Resthaven was a sprawling one-story building sitting unfenced on several acres of what could have been a park: rich green grass and flowers and small trees. I guessed the trees hadn't had time to get big. Everything looked new: clean and shiny and white. I glimpsed some little kids playing on a swing set, older ones shooting baskets.

"Not as bad as I thought," I said, half to myself, half to Lincoln. His hand closed on mine. His eyes were glued on the building as Buck pulled up in front and wedged the bulky sled into a spot designed for normal-sized cars.

He was out of the car before the engine died. I heard the trunk slam down, and a second later he was at my mom's door, suitcase in hand. He opened the door and helped her out.

"What are you waiting for, Petey?" he snarled.

"Judgment day."

"It's come and gone, boy."

Buck was right. And I'd been judged guilty.

Resthaven didn't smell as good as it looked. Once inside the double glass doors, I was reminded of school and cafeteria food and trips to the bathroom all rolled into one. And something else I didn't recognize at the time: disinfectant. The green, pukey-looking disinfectant cleaner I eventually saw them using on everything. As if whatever we inmates had was somehow catching.

We'd just set foot in the lobby when a man appeared out of nowhere and snatched my suitcase out of my hand.

"Let me help you with that, young fella," he said. He reached in his pocket, pulled out one of those plastic counters people use in grocery stores, and gave it a click. Everybody stopped and stared at him. Buck sidled over in front of Lincoln and my mom, as if the guy was going to attack them.

"Peter, is it?" the man asked. "We've been expecting you, Peter." He held his free hand out to me. A big tattoo of a scorpion barely showed against the dark brown skin of his forearm, which was thickly muscled and veined.

I stuck out my hand and watched it disappear in his. His grip was strong. The knuckles were big and knobby, as if they'd been broken once.

"Nice to meet you, Peter. I'm Scorpio."

"Your badge says Edward," I said.

He looked at his chest. "Right. My friends call me Scorpio."

"I'll call you Edward."

He laughed.

"*Peter*," my mom said. Buck rolled his eyes.

"No problem." Edward glanced from Buck to Lincoln. "I know you, don't I, young man? I've seen you on TV."

Lincoln held out his hand. "I'm Lincoln Champagne," he said, all grown-up-sounding.

Edward took his hand and pumped it up and down. "So this is one of those magic hands, huh?"

Lincoln shrugged.

"Tight end, Cowboys, about 2020, I'd say." Edward looked at Buck. "You're his famous dad."

Buck nodded and gave Edward his best car-salesman smile.

"We've got Peter's last name as Larson. I didn't realize you were his—"

"*Step*father," Buck and I said at the same time.

Edward studied our faces, maybe figuring that things weren't so great in our little family. "Uh-huh," he said. He shook hands with Buck and my mom. "Scorpio," he said loudly to each of them.

"You a doctor?" I asked.

He smiled. "Officially, I'm known as a tech. Unofficially, I'm the Resthaven greeter. I meet our new clients at the door. Make 'em feel at home."

"Right," I said. My mom gave me a look. Buck glanced at his watch and let out a loud sigh.

"You in a hurry?" Edward asked. Buck looked at his watch again. "Let me show you to Intake."

Across the big lobby a woman sat at a desk under a hanging sign that said Reception Area.

"I think we could've found it without your help," I told Edward as we walked up.

"Peter Larson," Edward said to the woman.

"Thanks for the introduction," I said.

Edward laughed. "No problem."

The woman smiled. "You're a little early, Peter."

I jerked my head toward my mom and Buck. "They didn't want me around any longer than I had to be."

"I'm sure they just wanted to be prompt. But in any case, if you and your family will have a seat, I'll call to see if Lila is ready to see you." She motioned toward a couch and some chairs.

We sat and waited. I closed my eyes, and when I opened them, Edward was gone. I closed them again, but I could feel Lincoln staring at me from close range. He was wedged up against me on the end of the couch.

I heard footsteps approach and stop. Lila, I figured. I opened my eyes the rest of the way and saw short gray hair surrounding a young smiling face. Each of her ears was dotted with four or five gold earrings. She stuck one hand out to me.

"Lila," she said. "It's good to meet you, Peter."

I stuffed my hands in my pockets.

"If you'd like to come with me for a few minutes, Peter, we can talk and give your parents a chance to get started on some paperwork." She handed my mom a stack of forms and a pen.

"I wouldn't like," I said.

My mom gave me a look again: disappointment, nervousness. I got up, and Lila offered me her hand once more: small, like the rest of her. She was five feet, tops—four or five inches shorter than me. I took her hand this time, surprised at her grip. I squeezed, harder and harder, but she just smiled and squeezed back until my knuckles ached. I eased off and she let go, still grinning.

"Nice firm handshake, Peter."

"Whatever."

Lila and I went to an office, where she asked me some familiar questions about school, friends, family, likes, dislikes, how I spent my time.

She left for a minute. When she got back, my mom and Buck were with her. Buck was looking bored, and my mom was still looking nervous.

"Where's Lincoln?" I didn't like the idea of him sitting by himself.

"He's fine. He's with Marianne," Lila said.

"You're pretending to care about him now, Petey?" Buck said, trying to make some kind of point. Lila ignored him. I ignored him.

"Sit down, please," Lila said to them, her voice as strong as her grip. For the next half-hour we answered Lila's questions. Forced to talk, my mom kept her answers short, checking most of them with glances at Buck.

I must have passed, or flunked, or whatever, because the last thing Lila did before we left the office was have my mom and Buck sign the papers to admit me.

Lila's phone rang just as we walked out the door. "Stay with them for a minute, will you, Scorpio?" she said to Edward, who'd reappeared. My suitcase rested between his two large shoes.

"You folks doing okay?" Edward asked.

"Great," I said.

"You'll get used to it, Petey." Buck was looking at his watch again.

"I'd rather not, Bucky."

Buck made a move toward me, but Edward stepped between us as quick and cool as a hailstone.

He crouched down, his back to Buck, his eyes boring into mine. "Why don't you and Lincoln take a little walk across the lobby, Peter, so you can tell each other good-bye."

I took Lincoln by the hand and headed across the lobby. When I looked back, Edward was standing tall and talking to Buck, real quiet like. From thirty feet away, I could only hear a low rumble, only see Edward's lips move. He and Buck were eyeing each other like two dogs with one bone. My mom looked real limp, hanging on Buck's arm like she was about to sag to the floor.

For a long minute Edward and Buck stood there, measuring each other, inside and out.

Lila walked out of the office. Buck's hands dropped to his sides. Edward picked up my suitcase and took something from his pocket. From across the room, I could hear the click of his counter. Lincoln's hand relaxed in mine.

"Come and kiss your momma good-bye, Petey," Buck called. But she was already heading toward me. I met her halfway, and she hugged me and kissed me. I smelled her perfume, and then she turned away, wiping at her eyes with her fist.

"Come on, Lincoln," she said.

But Lincoln pressed his face against my chest and held on. When I put my arms around him, I felt him crying. My throat lumped up, but I patted him on the back as if it was no big deal. "You'll see me before you know it."

He wouldn't let go, not until Buck came over, looked through me like I was window glass, and pried him away. "Let's go, Lincoln."

"See you, big guy," I said.

"Wednesday," my mom said. "We'll be back Wednesday. I'll call tonight to see how you're doing."

"Okay." I felt tears building up in my eyes.

"Or you can phone us." She handed me a piece of paper with their calling card number on it.

"Sure," I said.

They headed for the exit. Lincoln looked back once before Buck towed him through the door and out of sight.

"Ready, Peter?" Lila had a folder of papers in her hand. My folder, I guessed. I wondered what kind of lies were written in there.

Five

I followed Edward out of the lobby and through a big locked door marked Inpatient and Residential. Suddenly it grew graveyard quiet. The soft click of the door locking behind us sounded like a coffin lid slamming shut. I swallowed hard, trying to breathe.

Lila walked along at my side as we started down a long carpeted hallway lined with bright peach-colored walls. The first door on our right said Laundry. Across the hallway was one marked Housekeeping. Farther along were numbered, opened doors. I caught glimpses of furniture, but no people. We came to a room called Community, then a nurses' station. Two women and a man nodded to us as we walked by. On both sides of them were glass walls that separated them from the community room we'd passed and another one like it a few steps away. These rooms were unoccupied, too. I was wondering where the rest of the inmates were when we passed a closed door marked Group. Voices—a boy and girl, I figured, talking at the same time—floated through the heavy wood.

Edward waved at a door as we approached. "Men's room."

We went past more doors on both sides of the hallway. Finally we stopped in front of a door with the number 13 on it. "Your room, Peter." It figured. Edward stepped aside and motioned us past.

The room was bright, but the windows weren't very big. To my right, just inside the door, was a bathroom. Beyond the bathroom were two twin beds. Because of the way the bathroom stuck out into the room, I could only see the foot ends of the beds, but I could tell they were empty. Opposite the beds were two small desks, two chairs, and a closet. The walls were the same peach color, and everything was neat and clean. Sterile, almost. But at least the walls weren't rubber; I didn't see any fake mirror.

Edward carried my suitcase to the far bed. "We need to take a look-see through here with you, Peter." He spread the suitcase open like a clamshell, and he and Lila went through its contents piece by piece: jeans, shirts, shorts, socks, swimsuit, underwear, bathroom stuff, my book, a picture of Lincoln and me. Everything. Every pocket and corner and crevice of the suitcase probed and patted and undone and unfolded. Like my life.

I looked at all my stuff scattered across the bed, at Lila giving my suitcase another once-over, at Edward smelling my shampoo and opening my toothbrush container. "What are you looking for?"

"Contraband," Edward said. "Sharps."

Lila straightened up and smiled at me. "We just want to make sure there's nothing here that will hurt you or anyone else, Peter. Everyone who comes here has to go through this."

"It isn't right."

"It's for your own protection," Lila said. "We need to check you in at the nurses' station now."

Lila and Edward left me in the hands of a woman named Cat. Catherine D., R.N., her badge said. She was young, dark-haired, a little on the well-rounded side, a nice smile. Not much taller than Lila. We went to a room behind the nurse's station, where she put some stuff on a computer, weighed and measured me, and took my blood pressure and some blood. Then she sent me to a little bathroom to pee in a cup.

I came back out thinking they were going to know everything about me, and I was going to know nothing about them. I sat down at Cat's desk, watching her type. "Catherine's your real name?" I asked.

"Too big a mouthful for my brother when I was born. He called me Cat. It stuck."

"Too bad," I said, but secretly I liked it.

"It suits me." She smiled.

"So do you have a big litter box hidden around here somewhere?" I forced a laugh.

She laughed with me. "Right under the desk."

I leaned forward and almost peeked before she smiled again. "Ha-ha," I said.

She finished typing and handed me a sheet of paper. "You're probably wondering about your daily routine now that you're here, Peter."

"Not really."

"This is a schedule for a typical day. Not every day will be typical, but this will give you an idea."

One item caught my eye. "What's this three hours of school? It's the middle of summer."

"You get good grades in school, Peter?"

"They're okay."

"We'll try to make them better."

"Whatever."

Edward took me back to my room and left me. I closed the door behind him, surprised when it came right back at me. Edward swung it all the way into the room. "This door stays open at all times, Peter. You can use your bathroom to dress or undress, but the door to your room stays open."

"When I'm asleep?"

"Asleep, awake, night, day, whenever."

"You guys don't know about privacy?"

"It's a safety practice, Peter."

"Yeah." I walked to my bed and stared at my belongings. My clothes were folded neatly— better than I could have done—but I didn't like the idea that someone else had been messing with them. I could feel Edward's eyes on my back. I threw a pair of shorts against the wall and watched with satisfaction as they fell in a lump on the bed. When I turned around he was gone.

I put my stuff away. It didn't take long. I

wasn't sure what was supposed to happen next, but I figured they'd tell me.

I sat down on the bed with the only book I'd brought. I'd read *The Further Adventures of Hawk Ripley* often enough to know most of it by heart. The cover was faded and stained, the corners rounded. The pages were creased and wrinkled. But I never got tired of the story of the old magical cowboy, just as creased and wrinkled as the pages of the book, who rode into town to help out when the kid, Cole Crosby, was in trouble. I wasn't sure why I liked the book so much—maybe because Hawk wasn't riding into some Old West town. He rode his spotted horse Paint Bucket into Sludgeopolis, a modern city of cars and skyscrapers and crime.

I opened the book. The bookplate inside the front cover said, "To Peter, on your second birthday. Love, Mom." I tried to remember my second birthday, but drew a blank. I couldn't even recall my third or fourth. Worse, I had no recollection of my dad. Except for an image I'd conjured up in my own mind, I had no idea what he looked like.

I remembered turning five. It was the last year

before Buck came into the picture, riding up to the house in his big Lincoln, walking to the door holding his ten-gallon hat, as if he had manners. Shaking hands with me and smiling that car-salesman smile. He may have looked kind of like a cowboy, but even back then I knew he hadn't come to help me.

I heard voices out in the hall. A few seconds later a quick, shadowy movement caught my eye. I looked up. In the corner of the room, hidden from any passerby, stood a girl.

"Room service." Her voice was a woman's—deep and strong, but her body was a child's—skinny and weak. She tossed me an apple, which I managed to grab one-handed. She stood there, looking around the room.

"Nice view, New Guy," she said.

"Who are you?"

"Room service."

"Right."

"You depressed, New Guy?"

"Not till I got here."

"You look depressed."

"Who are you?"

"The prisoner Sarah."

"You supposed to be in this room?"

"They'll come and get me any minute. Eat your apple." She flopped down on the head of the other bed, still hidden from anyone in the hall by the L shape of the room. I watched a couple of boys—little ones—walk by outside the door and stare in at me.

"The Poet doesn't like me on his bed. Don't tell him."

"Who's the Poet?"

"Your roommate."

I looked at her, feeling stupid. Of course. A roommate called the Poet. What else could I have expected?

Sarah rolled onto her side, elbow on the bed, chin in her hand, and stared at me. Her eyes were dark and sunken in her narrow, angular face. Beneath her long-sleeved T-shirt and jeans she looked to be all bones. I guessed she was about my age.

"Why the Poet?"

She laughed, musical and throaty. "You'll see."

I couldn't wait. I looked back at my book,

hoping she'd go away. I didn't need someone laughing at me. But she didn't leave.

"Why are you here, New Guy?" She gave me her deep-eyed look.

Suddenly I felt tears coming and I turned, pretending to look out the window. I stared and blinked. "I don't know."

"That's what they all say."

"Are they coming to get you soon?"

"I've worn out my welcome already?"

"You never had one."

For what seemed like a long time, she didn't say anything, which was a relief. But then I heard a sob, followed by some full-blown crying. When I turned to look, she was face-down on the bed, her back quivering and quaking.

I got up and stood beside her. This was worse than dealing with Lincoln. "Sorry," I said, and put my hand on her shoulder. It felt as hard and knobby as a turtle shell.

She twisted onto her back. Her tearless eyes sparked with mischief. "Gotcha, New Guy!" She smiled. I didn't.

"My name's not New Guy."

Edward appeared from out of nowhere. "This your room, Sarah?"

"Maybe." She sat up and scooted to the edge of the bed.

"You could lose privileges for being in here."

"I was just saying hi to New Guy, Scorpio. I thought I was your assistant greeter."

"Only in the common areas. You know the rules."

"So, you gonna bust me?"

"You eat your apple?"

Sarah glanced at me; Edward's eyes followed. I lobbed the apple to him.

"Apple for the teacher?" Sarah asked.

He gave it back to her. "You need to eat this, or I'll talk to Cat."

Sarah took a small bite and made a face. She chewed like she'd bitten off a section of worm. Edward watched her until she swallowed.

"You gonna turn me in?"

"How much of that apple you gonna eat?"

"All of it?"

"Good answer. You eat all of it, I don't bust you."

"Can she eat it somewhere else?" I asked.

She took another bite, bigger, but didn't move. A kid—a boy about my age, but taller—walked into the room. He had long red hair pulled back in a ponytail and wore a black T-shirt that said POETRY IS LIFE. The Poet. It had to be. Too late, Sarah got to her feet. He had already spotted her. He put his hands on his hips and glared in her direction.

The eye, faster than the swiftest bird,
Catches the fledgling girl in mid-flight,
Sees the hollows and bumps on
Coverlet and pillow,
Remnants of the brash trespasser.

His words were rhythmic and measured and wrapped around long pauses. I could almost see the lines beginning and ending as his voice rose and fell and started and stopped. It was poetry. At least it sounded like it to me. Except it didn't rhyme.

"You crack me up, Eugene," Sarah said.

"It doesn't rhyme," I said. Eugene gave me a look.

"John," Edward said, trying to get his attention, but John/Eugene ignored him and stared past me, out the window.

"Eugene," Edward said, and John/Eugene looked at him. "This is your new roommate, Peter."

"Peter?" Sarah said. "What kind of poem can you make out of that, Eugene? Personally, I like 'New Guy' better."

Eugene studied me for a minute.

Face framed in fire, New Guy Peter
Stands within the walls of Rest Stop.
Sad-eyed here, lonely there,
Shadows in between.
Looking for a home,
A place where dreams come true.

Face framed in fire? What did he mean by that? I looked behind me. The early evening sky had turned dusty red, fiery. I wasn't sure about the rest of his poem. Eugene came over and offered me his hand. Real formal. I took it and we shook. He nodded, stepped back, and glanced from Sarah to Edward.

The star, still burning, nibbles, but
Will the fruit feed her flames,
Or come back, chunks
Of useless toilet art?

"She doesn't do that anymore, Eugene," Edward said. "And I'll make sure she eats the apple."

"But you're not busting me, right, Scorpio?"

"We'll see, Sarah. Come on." They headed for the door, Edward on Sarah's heels. She took another small bite before they turned down the hall. I heard the muffled click of Edward's counter.

"She doesn't eat?" I asked.

Eugene held his hand in the air, thumb and forefinger an eighth of an inch apart, before flopping on his bed. He pulled a notebook from under his pillow, propped his head on a hand, and started writing.

I sat down on my bed and looked at the paper Cat had given me. Edward kept wandering past our door, glancing in. At 5:30 he told us it was dinner time. I wasn't hungry.

Six

The cafeteria was in a separate wing of the building. We kids walked there as a group, Edward and Cat and another woman herding us along. Twenty of us or so, I figured. Most of them younger than me, a couple as young as Lincoln, probably.

Eugene walked through the food line in front of me, piling his plate high, then went to a small corner table where he sat by himself. I thought about joining him, but he didn't look up; he was writing furiously on a pad of paper. I figured he didn't want company.

I chose a table on the other side of the room, where two little kids—a boy and a girl—were sitting. The girl looked up and smiled when I sat down; the boy kept staring at his plate while he put his little finger in his nose, pulled out a pea-sized booger, and wiped it on his napkin. At least he hadn't eaten it.

I moved to an empty table and sat down facing the window, which looked out on a field and some trees. In the middle of the field was a basketball hoop surrounded by a slab of cement. To the left of the hoop, a metal fence formed a low border around a small swimming pool. Beyond the basketball court stood a swing set and a big wooden climbing toy.

Sarah set down her tray and sat across from me. "You want to be out there, New Guy?"

"Peter."

"Right. You want to be out there, Peter?"

"Anywhere but here."

"You get used to it."

"How long you been here?"

"A month, almost."

"For what?"

She looked at her plate, where her spaghetti sat untouched. "Eating disorder, they say."

"You don't eat enough?"

"So they say. Food sucks."

"You gotta eat."

"Why?"

I wasn't sure why. I'd tasted my food. It was okay, but I had a hard time getting it past the lump in my throat. "So you can go home," I said finally.

"That's a reason, anyway."

"You want to go home, right?"

"I miss it."

"Start eating."

She pushed her tray away. "What do *you* have to do to go home?"

I shrugged, but I had a pretty good idea: watch my mouth, quit fighting, play along. "I did some stuff; my parents thought I did some other stuff. I guess I need to get them to trust me. Somehow." I turned and looked across the room at Eugene. He was eating with one hand, writing with the other.

"Why's the Poet here?"

"Can't you tell?"

I shrugged again. I didn't think they'd lock you up for reciting poetry.

"Delusional behavior secondary to post-traumatic stress disorder with underlying major depression and anxiety." She sounded like she'd memorized the words for a chance to impress someone. I was impressed. "He thinks he's a famous poet named Eugene Rondeau," she said. "His name's John Hill."

"Delusional blah, blah, blah? Where'd you hear all that junk?"

She smiled. "I have my sources."

"How did he get like he is?"

"I guess he'd had some problems for a while; I don't know why. Then a drunk driver ran over his big brother. Killed him. Eugene couldn't handle it."

"Does he ever talk?"

"Like you and me?"

I nodded.

"Never. Just poetry. Half of it I don't get—like that one about you this afternoon."

Edward walked up with two dishes of tapioca pudding. "You guys forgot dessert," he said.

"We didn't forget, Scorpio," Sarah said. "That stuff looks like barf."

Edward put the dishes down between us. "I'll be standing right nearby, watching you eat." As he turned and walked away, he reached in his pocket. I thought I heard the click of his counter.

"What's his story?" I said.

"Ask him. He likes telling it."

Edward kept an eye on us, but he didn't come back to the table.

After dinner they let us go outside. The sun was nearly down to the treetops, but it was still hot. The other kids—most of them probably on one kind of drug or another—did a lot of sitting on the grass. But I'd been feeding my pills to the toilet for the past week or so; I felt better than I had for a long time. So this guy named Sam and I shot baskets.

Afterward I sat on the grass and dripped sweat. I thought about Lincoln and Tracy Ann and wondered if they were outside playing. Eugene paced around the field, writing on his pad. Sarah appeared from the shade of a big leafy tree and joined him. I could see her talking, but he didn't look up. She stayed at his side as he circled the field again and again. On the horizon behind them flame-fringed, ashy clouds, slow-dancing in waves of heat, hung over low, brown Texas hills. It was still hot when they took us back inside.

We all went into the room marked Group when we got back to our wing. We sat in chairs in a circle, and Lila introduced me. Some of the kids looked at me, some looked through me, some didn't even look. We were supposed to be talking about how things were going on the wing, who was doing what right and wrong, how to make things work better, all that stuff.

The kid who'd been mining boogers—his name was Ethan—got up and did a strange, twirling, silent dance. I didn't say anything when it was my turn. But Lila waited, not calling the next name.

"You're new here, Peter," Cat said from the doorway. "We'd like to hear what you think of Resthaven."

"I'll take a rain check."

"Tomorrow, maybe," Lila said.

"The food sucks," Sarah said when her turn came.

"What kind of food would you like?" Cat asked.

"None."

Lila kept going around the circle until she came to Eugene. "John?" she said. He stared at the floor silently, as if he hadn't heard a thing. "Eugene?" she said, and he raised his face to the fading light outside the big window.

Words sown in the fertile dark of silence
Need room to grow and flower.
Burdened by noise, crowded, they
Stunt and shrivel
And lie brown and dormant,
Waiting for space and twilight, for the
Passing of the outsider called Peter.

I didn't get all of Eugene's poetry, but I figured out he didn't want me in his room.

"You might like having a roommate, Eugene," Lila said. "Peter's a nice guy, he's quiet. You'll still have your own space. Right, Peter?"

"If there's anything I like to eat," I said, "it's paper. Especially stupid little note pads of yellow paper with stupid, unrhymed poems written on them. I eat it for breakfast, lunch, and dinner, and I can sniff it out no matter where it's hiding."

Eugene pulled his note pad to his chest and stared at me, eyes wide. I made a move toward him, and he scrambled from his chair. I pulled a piece of paper napkin from my pocket, stuffed it in my mouth, and started to chew. It tasted like spaghetti and tapioca pudding.

"Sit down, please, Peter," Edward said, and I felt his hands, like slabs of meat, on my shoulders. I sat down.

"Peter's joking, Eugene," Lila said. "Please sit down. You *are* joking, right, Peter?"

"Maybe." I spit out the napkin. Eugene looked a little calmer.

We kept going around the circle until it got back to Lila. She talked about some stuff that had happened that day—a kid had run down the hall and tried to unlock the fire exit door. Two kids had gotten in a fight in the community room, and the TV had to be turned off. Some beds weren't made. Clothes weren't put away. And someone had drawn a body part on the little man on the men's room door. Some of the young kids giggled at the last announcement—all but Ethan, who just stared at the floor. Lila didn't say anything about Sarah, or anyone, going to someone else's room.

Lila asked for comments. She got a few. Eugene avoided me on the way out. But when I growled at him, I thought I saw a little smile.

We went to one of the community rooms. We voted on a TV show while a food service woman rolled in a cart full of fruit. I grabbed some grapes and sat down in a stuffed chair. My mouth was still dry from the napkin.

Sarah sat next to me, empty-handed. But in a minute Cat handed her a banana, half-peeled. "I'm going to watch you eat this, Sarah."

"You planning on being here a while?"

"As long as it takes."

Sarah took a nibble of banana.

Buck's commercial came on the TV, and there he was, smiling that phony smile, telling those lies. I was close enough to spit at him, but I held myself back. I didn't want to be the subject of the next community get-together; I didn't want to lose privileges, whatever those were.

Buck tossed the football, and Lincoln appeared magically on the screen, leaping to catch the ball. I wished that I could be the one making the throw, that Lincoln and I—just the two of us—were out tossing the ball around the backyard, that he was giving me his big smile.

The little kids sitting in front of the set perked up. Lincoln snagged the big ball with one hand and brought it in to his chest before dunking it through the open window of the car chosen as the Jumbo Deal of the Week. The camera zoomed in on his smile as he landed on the ground, and it backed off as he did his little dance.

"That's my brother," I said, mostly to myself.

"Your brother?" Sarah said. "Really? It looks like *he* doesn't miss many meals."

"He's going to be a football player," I said.

"That guy's your dad?"

"*Step*dad."

"Oh. Well, that's good. He looks a little slick."

"Yeah."

My mom called a while later. A tech named Walter came and took me to the nurses' station, where a pay phone hung on the wall. It was good hearing from my mom, but I couldn't really listen to what she was saying. Her voice rose and fell with that fake cheer she used whenever Buck was around. I asked to talk to Lincoln.

"I just saw you on TV, big guy."

"I miss you, Peter."

"Mom's coming Wednesday. Maybe you can come, too."

"How many days?"

"About three."

"Three's a lot."

"Not really." But right then it seemed like a life-time to me.

My mom took back the phone. I could hear Lincoln protesting, then crying, in the background. We said good-bye and Walter escorted me back to the community room. A few minutes later Sarah walked in. She picked up a magazine and plopped down next to me on the couch, chewing seriously on her gum but smelling of something else.

"They let you smoke here?"

She gave me a grin. "Good nose."

"You smell like an ashtray."

"It's something to do besides eat."

"They let you?"

"As long as I don't get caught."

What surprised me was that she'd found a place where she could be alone long enough to light up a cigarette. I felt like someone had had me under a microscope since I'd checked in.

The surveillance didn't stop after I went to bed. The lights were off in our room, but the hallway light shone through the open door, and every few minutes one of the techs came in far enough to make sure Eugene and I were still there and behaving ourselves. No wild parties allowed. No early checkout from that hotel.

Eugene fell asleep fast. I heard his breathing even out and slow. I wondered about his dreams. Would they be in poetry?

I couldn't imagine him having dreams like mine, which these days were often about my dad. He had somehow survived the shipwreck and returned, full of life, full of love for me. We were always together, doing something fun: playing catch, shooting hoops, canoeing across a mountain lake. Sometimes my mom would be in the dream, too, and I'd study them as they laughed together. When the dream ended, I'd wake up crying, fighting to remember my dad's face. But the best I could ever do was a fuzzy, grown-up version of myself.

Half asleep, I heard Eugene stir and make a noise. The shadowy figure of a man came through the door and went to Eugene's bed. The man pulled up the covers and tucked them in around Eugene's shoulders. I heard a familiar click. Sleep came.

Seven

We got up early the next day—too early for the middle of summer. But we had a load of stuff to do: make our beds, shower, pick up our clothes, take our pills, eat breakfast, go to class. And that was just in the morning.

I didn't recognize any of the people working the early shift, but they seemed to know who I was. A nurse named Claire brought Eugene and me our pills. But she called him John, and while they were trying to straighten out that misunderstanding, I palmed my pills and slipped them in my pocket. On my next trip to the bathroom they took a ride down the yellow river.

I ate breakfast with Eugene, Sam, and a couple of younger kids. Sarah had to sit at a table by herself while a woman tech named Leslie hovered over her, watching her eat.

I really wasn't ready for school, but that's what we did after breakfast. The teacher was a young guy named Mitch who was tall enough to have been a basketball player. He had me start out by choosing a book from the library and reading it while the other kids began their lessons. He gave me some tests to take—to see where I was academically, he said—and that took up most of the remaining time. The three hours went pretty fast, but Mitch said I'd get started on some real stuff the next day.

Just as class was ending Leslie came and got me. Phone call, she said. She walked me to the nurses' station. I could feel her eyes on me as I picked up the phone.

"Hello," I said.

"Peter?" The voice was young and soft, almost a whisper.

"How you doin', Lincoln?"

"Okay." He didn't sound okay.

"Is Mom there, Lincoln?"

"No."

"Who is?"

"Rosie."

The babysitter. "Where's Rosie?"

"Downstairs."

"You called me all by yourself, Lincoln?"

"Your number's on the refrigerator. I had a dream last night, Peter."

"A real dream?"

"Yes."

"What about, Lincoln?"

"The man with wings."

"The man with wings dream is real?"

"Yes. Dad says there's no such thing as real dreams. He told me not to talk about 'em."

"What was the man doing in this dream?"

"Running."

"Running? Why not flying?"

Lincoln laughed. "Not those kinds of wings, silly."

"What kind?"

"Little ones. On his shirt."

"On his shirt? He was wearing them?"

"Like a badge."

"So why was he running? Was he chasing someone?"

"Not chasing. Hurrying. There were lots of people, and airplanes on the ground outside."

"An airport? Was it an airport?"

"Maybe."

I felt a hand on my shoulder. "Just a second, Lincoln." I turned to face Leslie.

"You're late for lunch, Peter. You'll have to talk later." She didn't look ready to negotiate.

"I gotta go, Lincoln. Call me the next time Rosie's there."

"What does it mean, Peter?"

"I don't know. I'll think about it. Bye, Lincoln."

By the time I got to lunch, most people were working on dessert. Eugene had eaten everything but his corn and peas, which he was arranging in alternate rows—peas, corn, peas—in the center of his plate. As usual, Sarah's plate was full, but she'd done a pretty good job of spreading her food around. Just as I sat down, she reached over with her fork and swiped across Eugene's rows of green and yellow.

Without looking up, he started arranging them again. A few seconds later, he spoke.

Don't send your fork on a jester's journey,
For it has real business, serious and urgent.
Your life-fire is starving, it must be fed,
Or the house of Sarah will burn itself down.

"You think I'm gonna starve myself to death, Eugene?" Sarah sounded angry and scared.

Eugene picked up the straw from his carton of milk and bent it in the middle until it collapsed.

"I'm not," Sarah said. "I'm *not!*"

Eugene took his fork to Sarah's plate and pushed her food around until it was a barfy-looking mess of corn and peas and applesauce and mashed potatoes and gravy and cottage cheese. He tossed his fork at her plate and watched it bounce to the floor. Then he went back to arranging his rows.

Leslie walked over and looked at the mess on Sarah's plate. "I'll get you some fresh food," she said.

Sarah sat and stared at her plate when it came back. She was still sitting when the rest of us went out to the yard. From outside I saw Leslie standing over Sarah like some kind of judge.

After our recess most of the kids went to group sessions; I went to my room. They hadn't assigned me to a group yet. I'd just opened my book when Edward walked in.

"On your own for a while, Peter?"

"I *was.*"

"What are you reading?"

"*Hawk Ripley*," I said. "It's about a cowboy."

He patted a box that he carried under his arm. "How about chess?" he asked.

I said okay. I didn't tell him I'd taken third place in a chess tournament when I was in sixth grade. I hadn't played much since then. We sat down on the bed and opened the board between us. His men were heavy onyx, the colors of moss and waterfalls. I took the waterfall color and went first, eager to show my skill. But four moves later it was over, and Edward wore a smile.

"A little rusty, I guess," he said, and I nodded.

But the next game he began giving me tips. By the seventh or eighth game I was hanging in there. Edward still had me on the run, he still beat me, but not as quick and easy.

After another half-dozen games, still unthreatened, he stood. "Got things to do. You want, we'll go at it again tomorrow." He put the chessmen gently in the box, closed the lid, and then reached in his pocket. I heard the click of his counter as he turned for the door.

I couldn't take it. "Why do you do that? You keeping track of your hours or something?"

Edward smiled. "Not exactly," he said. "I count my good deeds."

"What good deed did you just do?"

"The chess game. Playing chess with you."

"I thought I was doing *you* the favor."

"You can count it, too."

"Why would I *want* to? Why would *you* want to?"

Edward came back and sat on the bed. He looked at his watch. "I'll give you the short version." His body seemed to relax, and he got this dreamy look on his face. "Sister Moses. Preacher lady. A beautiful preacher lady."

A couple of years before, said Edward, he'd met a woman who invited him to a tent revival. "I was inside, enjoying the music but mostly wondering how much longer before we could leave. Then Sister Moses came on stage and started preaching. She had the face of an angel and a voice like honey.

"She talked about the choices we make in life. About how God keeps this tally book with all the things people have done. At the end of our time on earth He adds up all the good and bad things to see what side of the ledger we come down on."

"Did you believe her?"

"I didn't want to, but I couldn't help myself. And when she finished preaching, she started singing, and it was like my feet were lifted off the ground. Her voice came from her soul and poured out the music, like wind chimes in a July breeze. I forgot that girl sitting next to me, I forgot everything but Sister Moses. Folks started moving toward that stage and I went with them, not even knowing what I was doing.

"I knelt down before her, staring straight ahead, afraid to look up. But she took my chin in her hand and raised it, and I looked into those eyes and she looked inside mine, way inside. She saw me for what I was—a sinner—but she smiled and raised me up and sang a verse of 'Amazing Grace' in that beautiful voice, and then she hugged me. She rocked me like a baby.

"After too short a time she let me go. But I kept watching her. She touched everyone who came past, but she only hugged the children." Edward's dreamy look turned dreamier. "She only hugged the children.

"I went back on my own the next day, but

the tent was gone. Everything was gone. As if I'd imagined the whole thing. But it wasn't my imagination. And I made up my mind. I was going to be a better man. I was going to put that tally book in better shape." He held up the counter. "I quit my job as a bouncer, I quit hanging out with losers, I got some more schooling, I moved. I started doing good things and keeping track."

"How do you know when you'll be ahead?"

"I figured I was ten or eleven years old before I did anything bad enough to count. I figured one or two bad things a week for nearly twenty years is roughly a couple thousand. I added another thousand to cover the worst ones. I figured I had to do at least three thousand good things to get myself on the right side of that tally book."

"You do good stuff *just* so you can count it?"

"And I like it. I've gotten to like it."

"So you'd play chess with me even if you didn't get to write it down as a good deed?"

"I like playing chess. I like you."

"The answer's yes?"

"I'd still play. You don't want me to count it next time, I won't count it." He shoved the counter into his pants pocket and then held out his big hands to me, palms up. "I won't take the counter out of my pocket. I won't even touch it." His smile couldn't hide the disappointment in his eyes.

"Count what you want. But you should probably be hanging around someone else. I won't be needing much in the way of good deeds."

Edward got to his feet. "I'll take my chances."

"The tally book—you're getting close?"

"Closer." He headed for the door. "See you."

"Later," I said.

He turned back, a question on his face. "Where you from, Peter?"

"Why?"

"The way you say some of your words sounds not quite Texas."

"Here. I'm from here."

Edward shrugged. "Just curious."

Eight

"How are you doing so far, Peter?" Lila looked at me over the tops of her reading glasses.

"Great."

"Being treated okay?"

"Like a prince."

"We'll have to get you a crown."

"And a ticket out of here."

"Where would you go, Peter?"

"I don't know."

"Home?"

"Maybe."

"Do they treat you like a prince there?"

"More like Cinderella."

I expected her to tell me I was wrong, that I had no reason to feel like that. "Why do you think you're treated that way?" she asked.

I told her. I talked while she mostly listened.

She wanted to know more about my mom and Buck and school and my friends. She asked me about Lincoln.

I told her Lincoln was a bit of a pain at times, but he was the best thing about my family. He was special. I didn't tell her all the reasons he was special.

"What about your father?" Lila asked. I stared at her for a second or two. We'd just gotten done talking about Buck. "Your real father. What do you know about him?"

"Not much. My mom doesn't talk about him."

"Have you asked her?"

"I used to."

"What did she tell you?"

"He was a commercial fisherman. He died in a boat accident off the Gulf Coast."

"Was that difficult for you?"

"I don't remember."

"You were how old?"

"Almost two, I guess."

"It was hard on your mom, I bet."

"They were already divorced."

Lila cleared her throat and wrote something on

her paper. "You moved from Corpus Christi to Deadwood then? You and your mom?"

"I guess. We've lived there as long as I can remember."

"You have relatives there?"

"No."

"None?"

"Buck's relations is all."

"No grandparents? Aunts? Uncles? Cousins?"

"I used to wish for some whenever I had a birthday. I used to pray for some at night. But my mom and dad had no brothers or sisters. Their parents are dead. My mom told me to pray for something else."

"So it was just you and your mom for a while."

"Till I was five or six."

"And then things changed for you."

"Thanks to Buck."

Lila wrote some more. Finally she got up and smiled.

"Thanks for coming, Peter."

"I had a choice?"

"You always have a choice."

"I'll remember that."

Lila walked me to the nurses' station and left. I sat while Cat looked through a short stack of papers and put them in my file.

"Your exam results look great, Peter: blood pressure, blood, urine, weight, all that stuff. No bugs, no drugs. You take good care of yourself."

"I try."

"You've been on your meds for a while now?"

"A while." I figured she was going to ask me if I was taking them.

"Good. As you know, we keep your meds and hand them out to you as they're needed, but with older kids like you, it's kind of an honor system."

What was she expecting me to do? Confess that I wasn't taking my pills?

"We wouldn't monitor meds that closely unless we thought they weren't being taken."

"Makes sense."

She looked at me for a few seconds. "Based on your behavior, we have no reason to think you're skipping your medicine. You're one of the coolest kids I've seen. Still, there's something I need to talk to you about."

"What's that?"

"Your lab tests indicate that you haven't been taking your meds."

"I guess I forgot for a few days."

"Claire gave them to you today, though, right?"

"Yes." I didn't tell Cat what I'd done with them.

"Good. That will be a good way to remember, won't it?"

"Yes."

"Because it's important that you take your meds until your doctor decides they're no longer necessary."

"But I'm doing okay without the pills. You said so yourself. Can you tell that to Dr. Lubber?"

"I'll pass it on, Peter. But in a few days we'll run another test to check your levels again. By then they should be approaching expected concentrations."

I got her meaning: take your pills. I was ready for a new subject.

"What about the other kids in this place? What happens to kids once they leave here?"

"They usually don't leave until we think they're better. A lot of times they stay better. They don't have to come back."

"What about Sarah? Eugene?"

"I've seen a lot worse."

"Did they get better?"

"Some." Cat wasn't going to give away any secrets. "That's good," I said.

When I finished up with Cat, it was time for swimming. I couldn't wait to hit the water, to wash away that feeling of being locked up and examined and inspected. And found out. Now I was going to have to decide whether to keep flushing the pills.

I walked out next to Eugene and Sarah. He had his hair ponytailed back with a rubber band. Hers was straight and dark and shiny. But I couldn't help staring at her legs. Below her long T-shirt they moved like fleshy bones, every joint and muscle and blood vessel showing. When we got inside the pool gate and she took off her shirt, it was worse. Her black one-piece suit hung on her like a drape, drooping from her shoulders, bunching up against the bones of her hips.

"What are you looking at, New Guy?"

"A skeleton."

She turned her back, dove into the water, and surfaced on the other side of the pool. She held on to the edge, facing away, while most of the other kids jumped or waded in. Eugene stood and shrugged his freckled shoulders at me.

Sarah looks, the mirror lies,
She sees another through her eyes.
Skin and bone is where she's at,
But where you see thin, she sees fat.

"A real poem, Eugene. Rhymes and everything."

Heed the words, not the rhyme,
Help her while she still has time.

Eugene jumped into the pool and swam over to Sarah. I dove in and headed for the bottom, to the deepest part, before my ears and chest started aching. I surfaced and swam laps until my arms were tree-trunk heavy and both calves were cramped. In the water no one could see my tears.

Nine

In bed that night I opened my book, anxious to lose myself in *The Further Adventures of Hawk Ripley*. Eugene, propped up on his pillow, closed his writing tablet and looked over at me. I began reading and glanced back. He was still staring.

"You want me to read it out loud?"

He nodded. For just a second I saw the beginnings of a smile. His eyes, even across the room, took on some extra life.

I read for a half-hour, probably. Finally we got to the part where Hawk arrives at Cole's house to find him missing. All that's there is a note from the Sludgeopolis crime lords telling Hawk to get out of town or he'll never see Cole alive again.

Eugene was sitting on the edge of his bed now, riding on every word. But my sixth-grade teacher had taught me one thing about out-loud reading: always keep the audience hanging. So

I closed up the book and put it under my pillow.

Eugene looked like he was going to protest, but he either changed his mind or couldn't come up with another poem quick enough. He turned off his light, I turned off mine, and a little later I heard his breathing, regular and peaceful, rising above the dead-soul quiet of Resthaven.

Sleep didn't come for me. I listened to Eugene; watched out of the corner of my eye as Edward patrolled past the door; stared at the shadowy ceiling. Finally I switched on my lamp, retrieved *Hawk*, and opened it up. I saw the bookplate with my mom's inscription inside the front cover, mocking me with its false-hearted message: "To Peter, on your second birthday. Love, Mom." One corner of the plate was peeled back a fraction of an inch. Temptingly peeled back.

I didn't want to look at the words any longer. I pulled, and the plate tore away cleanly.

I expected to find a blank spot, but something else was written right where the bookplate had been: "Happy second birthday, Peter. May all your trails be happy. We love you. Dad and Mom."

I stared at the words, reading and rereading.

Dad and Mom? They were already divorced when I turned two. My dad was already *dead* when I turned two. I combed my brain, looking for an explanation. Was that what my mom had told me, or was it just what I remembered? Did he die *before* I turned two, or *when* I was two? If he'd still been alive on my second birthday, would they have bought a gift together if they were divorced? Was the note on top a phony? Was my mom hiding something from me? What was it?

I felt like I'd jumped into another world, but I was surrounded by fog. If the bookplate message was a lie, what else was?

"Lights out, Peter," Edward said from the doorway. His voice came to me softly, but I jumped, shaken loose from my thoughts. I switched off the light, then slipped the wrinkled bookplate inside the cover of *Hawk*.

I stretched out, my body tingly, my head full. Wide awake, I lay in the half-dark, asking myself questions, struggling for answers.

Ten

In the dream, my mom was shaking me awake for school. Somehow I knew it was a dream, but it seemed real, too.

Sarah was kneeling at my bedside. I could just make out her silhouette, pencil-thin against the light from the door.

"You awake, New Guy?" Her whisper smelled like toothpaste.

"I am now." Barely awake. The inscription in *Hawk* had kept me tossing and turning for what seemed like hours.

"I couldn't sleep. Wanna come with me?"

"Where?"

"I'll show you. But first you gotta make it look like you're still in bed. Stuff your pillow down here."

I did what she said, wedging my pillow under the bedding and down towards the foot of the bed. Then we headed for the door.

She peeked into the hall. "Come on."

The emergency exit was wide open to the black night air. I heard music coming from the nurses' station up ahead. "Where's the tech?" I whispered.

Sarah didn't answer. She pushed open the door to the girls' bathroom and went in.

I was wearing shorts and a T-shirt, but I felt naked standing in the corridor. I followed her.

Sarah went to the last stall and climbed on the toilet. She stood on her toes and reached up to where a metal grill was fastened to the ceiling. She used a dime to loosen its two screws, and when the grill dropped down, she removed a pack of cigarettes and some matches.

She hopped off, popped a cigarette in her mouth, and held out the open pack to me. I took one, checked real casual-like to make sure I had the right end, and stuck it expertly between my lips. I'd seen a lot of other people smoking. She smiled and lit a match like she'd done it a thousand times before. She lit my cigarette, then hers. I took a big puff and breathed the smoke into my lungs as if it was pure, sweet air. I felt like I was swallowing my tongue.

I blew the smoke out, trying not to cough or

sneeze or throw up. I felt sick. "You really like these things?" I flipped my cigarette toward the toilet, and it hit the water with a hiss.

"It's an acquired taste."

"So's skunk meat."

She inhaled. I could see her ribs against her shirt, and I imagined the smoke somewhere inside her, looking for space in that skinny body. She blew another gray cloud in my direction.

"Where's the tech?" I asked again.

She jerked her head in the general direction of the emergency exit. "Out having a smoke. He spends more time outside than in."

"Why doesn't the alarm sound?"

"He turns it off."

"You can do that?" I could see myself heading out that lonesome door and not coming back. But where would I go? Home, where only Lincoln wanted me? Or somewhere else. Anywhere else.

"He has a key. I've seen him use it."

"Does he ever just leave the door open?"

"Only when he's out there."

So much for me heading out the door. "Who's at the nurses' station?"

"Tonight it's Weber. You planning to leave?"

"Never. I love it here."

She offered me her cigarette, and I saw a faint reddish smudge on the filter end. She was wearing lipstick. "Try again?"

The flowery taste of lipstick hit me like a gust of sweet Texas wind. I took a drag, sucking the perfumy smoke into my lungs.

The cough started somewhere deep inside me and erupted explosively. I bent over and tried to muffle the sounds with my shirt.

Sarah returned the pack to its hiding spot. The dime flashed as she drove the screws through the grill. From where I stood, everything looked untouched. She went to the door and peeked. "Still outside. You better be getting back, New Guy."

I slipped out, watching the doorway at the end of the hall through watery, blurry eyes. I got into my room before I heard the sound of a door closing. I was in bed when the tech glanced in.

I kept listening. The silhouette of the tech appeared in the doorway a few more times. A little while later I heard noises—keys, the big bar latch being pushed. I imagined the door opening to the night air once more.

A few seconds later another shape showed up at my door. Sarah gave me a thumbs-up sign, and I returned it. She flitted away like a moth, heading toward her room. I stayed awake for a while, the taste of sweet-scented smoke in my mouth.

Eleven

The next morning started off okay. Claire brought us our pills, but while Eugene was washing his down with a drink of water, he went into this choking fit. For just a moment Claire turned her attention to him, but it was long enough. I pocketed my pills, cupped my empty hand against my mouth, then took a long drink of water. Eugene, suddenly recovered, snuck me a smile.

Breakfast and school came next. Not too bad, but then things got worse. Dr. Lubber showed up, and one of his scheduled victims was me. As I walked into his office, I told myself to behave.

"Sit down, Peter." He was glancing through some papers. I took a seat in a chair that was half a foot shorter than his—a little kid's chair. I felt like I was looking up at the Emperor of Resthaven.

He put the papers in a neat little stack and stared at me from on high.

"Hello up there," I said.

"You look tired, Peter."

"I feel fine."

"Sleeping well?"

"Great. And you?"

"Your records indicate you've done well since your arrival, but your success may not continue if you don't take your medications regularly."

"How much longer do I have to take them?"

"That remains to be seen, but it would be helpful for you to adjust your thinking on the subject. If a carpenter is repairing a house, and he wants to do the best job possible, he would use all the tools in his toolbox. He wouldn't pound nails with his fists. Medications are simply useful tools, essential in some cases."

"So now you're a carpenter?"

"Of sorts."

"And I'm the ramshackle house."

He leaned forward, pushed his glasses to the tip of his nose, and peered down at me. "I see your talent for cynicism hasn't left you, Peter."

"Most of us have some kind of talent."

He sat back. "Have you had a chance to

think about your feelings for Lincoln?"

"I think he's a great kid. Same as always."

"When he gets favored treatment? How does that make you feel? Do you feel jealous?"

"Some. But that's not Lincoln's fault."

He wrote something on a piece of paper. "Whom do you blame?"

"Buck. My mom."

"Uh-huh. And do you plan on doing anything about it?"

"I have no plans. Period."

"What I hear you saying is that you feel you're being mistreated, but you have no design for getting back at the people who are abusing you."

"You heard me saying that because that's what I said."

"That's hard to believe, in light of your history. You've attempted to get back at your parents by hurting Lincoln."

"We're done with our little talk."

"We have more to discuss."

I sat as tall as I could in my baby chair and gave him a look, long and silent.

"You're not doing yourself any favors, Peter."

"You're lucky Hawk isn't around."

"Who?"

"Never mind." I looked out the window at the low, bare hills in the distance, hoping to spot a lone rider heading out of a secret canyon. He'd be crouching flat against the wind, and old Paint Bucket would be flying, trailing a cloud of dust.

After a few more minutes of silence, Lubber picked up his phone and pushed some buttons. "Peter's ready for you."

When Leslie came, Lubber smiled and offered me his hand. "It's been good visiting with you, Peter."

Not to be out-phonied, I smiled back. "The pleasure's been all mine."

After lunch, I had an appointment with Lila. She didn't have a file in front of her. Just Lila and me and some questions. Not even hard questions. Mostly stuff we'd already talked about the day before. But I was having a hard time concentrating on our conversation; I kept thinking about my dad. The note in *Hawk* was like the most exciting, edge-of-my-seat movie ever, and Lila's voice faded to background noise—like my mom's voice telling me to clean my room.

"What are you thinking, Peter?" I heard her say through the darkness of my private theater.

I shrugged. "My dad," I said finally.

"Do you miss him?"

"I didn't even know him."

"That doesn't matter. You miss knowing him. You miss his presence. It can be just as hard."

She was right; I felt cheated, abandoned. "I wish I could remember him."

"You have photos, at least."

"Stolen. All our pictures were stolen when we moved to Deadwood."

"That's too bad. It would be nice for you to be able to see what he looked like."

"Yeah."

"Especially now, when you need to believe you have someone on your side."

I shrugged again. Having a dead guy on my side—even if it was my dad—didn't seem like much help.

"You have people on your side here, you know, Peter," I heard her say, but her voice faded out again as my thoughts rewound to the phony bookplate. When did my dad really die? How? And finally, the one idea that kept flaming up from a dark corner of my mind: If my mom had lied about *when*, could she have lied about the whole thing? *Did* he die?

"Peter?" Lila leaned close, staring into my eyes.

"Uh-huh?" I doused the flickering thoughts of my dad. I couldn't afford to get my hopes up.

"Did you hear what I said about the people here?"

"Yeah."

"You don't know us very well, but we want to help you. We'll do whatever we can."

She looked like she meant it. "Thanks," I said. By the time I left her office, I felt better than I had since I'd gotten to Resthaven.

They put me in Group with Sarah, Eugene, and Sam, probably because we were the oldest on the wing. We didn't have much else in common.

Lila had just asked Eugene to tell us what was on his mind when Sam got up from his chair and started walking around the room. Eugene stayed focused, ignoring Sam, even though he was walking faster, circling our chairs like an orbiting spacecraft. I could see Eugene's mind playing with the question, cooking up a poem.

"Sam—" Lila said.

Sam stopped, took a baseball out of his pants pocket, and chucked it at one of the big windows, ten feet away from where he stood.

Glass exploded. Most of it flew out, but some big chunks hung in the air for a second, then fell straight down and shattered against a table. I ducked, but I couldn't take my eyes away from the jagged hole in the window as everything seemed to drift along in slow motion. Glass fell; Sarah dove to the floor; Eugene looked up, eyes wide.

Lila picked up a phone and punched in some numbers. Sam just stood there, a strange expression—wonder, maybe—on his face. In the background an alarm sounded, loud and steady.

The door flew open, and Cat ran in with Edward on her tail. They stopped on either side of Sam and checked out the damage.

"Looks like a fast ball to me, Sammy," Edward said. "High and outside."

"Got away from me."

"Lots of speed, though," Edward said.

Cat turned to Sam. "You take your pills today?"

Sam looked away from the window for the first time. "No."

"How about yesterday?"

Sam shook his head.

"Let's go for a walk," Cat said, and led Sam from the room.

That was about it for Group. Edward and Lila took us back to our rooms. Eugene had some extra time to come up with a poem, which he recited as soon as we were alone.

> Slingin' Sammy, the king of cool,
> Takes the heat off the poetry guy,
> Beats the boredom of the mind-game school
> With a whistling fast ball, hard and high.
> Sam says dump 'em if you dare,
> The deer in the fields don't take pills.
> Let the Rest Stop powers that be beware:
> Words and potions don't cure all ills.

"That's a good one, Eugene. You gonna write it down?"

He held up his notebook and a pen. He started

writing just as Edward came back with a message for me: I had a phone call.

✳

There was a pause after I said hello, and then Lincoln's voice, nearly a whisper.

"Are you smoking?" He sounded like I'd just wrecked his best toy and tried hiding it from him.

"I was just playing around, Lincoln. Just once."

"You won't do it again?"

I thought of the taste of Sarah's lipstick. "Probably not."

"Promise?"

"Okay."

He took a breath, and his voice got even softer. "Who was that skinny girl?"

"Her name's Sarah."

"Do you like her?"

"I guess."

"Are you going to marry her?"

"I think you better get off, now, Lincoln."

He protested, but I reminded him that I'd see him the next day, and he finally hung up.

Between swimming and dinner my mom called.

She told me Lincoln missed me. She said she was looking forward to our visit the next day. She didn't mention Buck.

I coasted through dinner and Community and Rec. I couldn't stop thinking about Lincoln and his amazing gift. What would it be like to have that power? Exciting? Scary? Both, I figured. And more.

When I got to room 13, Eugene was already in bed, sitting up, staring at me, arms folded across his chest.

"You waiting for more *Hawk*, Eugene?"

He smiled. He had a good smile. I hadn't seen it much.

I read for almost an hour. In the near-dark I could imagine being somewhere else: walking a dusty trail and then leaving it far below, floating above everything, watching the world drift by beneath me as I headed toward a blue, blue mountain lake in the distance.

I stopped reading when my eyes wouldn't stay open any longer. I could see Eugene, still sitting up waiting for more, but when I closed the book he settled back. I turned off my reading lamp and for the first time beat him to sleep.

Twelve

Sarah was waking me up again. I almost told her to go away. Almost. But I got up, and we crept to the girls' bathroom like worms escaping from a birdhouse.

Sarah got down her pack of cigarettes and offered me one.

I shook my head. "That's okay," I whispered.

"Why not?" She lit one, inhaled, and waited for my answer. When she exhaled she held the cigarette close to her face, and the glow put some pink in her pale cheeks.

"Why not?" she repeated.

"I promised my brother I wouldn't."

She took another drag. "You told him you were smoking last night?"

"Not exactly."

"You didn't tell him you were smoking, but he made you promise not to smoke again?"

I explained things to her—everything about

Lincoln's real dreams. Sarah took one last drag and pitched it toward the toilet. It seemed to sail in slow motion, painted with a bright smudge of lipstick. It hit the water with a quick pop.

She opened her mouth in a little O and blew five donut-sized smoke rings in my direction. Then she put the back of her hand on my forehead.

"No fever, New Guy. And that's *not* good news."

"What do you mean?"

"You were the one person I couldn't figure. I mean, why were you here? Now I know."

"I didn't make this up."

We stood there for a minute, not saying anything. The bathroom was hot. I thought Sarah and I were friends, kind of, but she didn't believe what I'd told her. To her I was just another goofy kid with delusions.

"You look sad, New Guy."

"I'm tired."

"I'm sorry for what I said."

"No problem."

She put her hand on my forehead again. It felt cool. "You ever kissed a girl, New Guy?"

"Lots of times."

"You like it?"

"Sure."

"You want to kiss me?"

Suddenly I felt warmer. I'd never come close to kissing a girl. I didn't know what to say.

"Well?" She stepped closer to me and moved her hand to my shoulder. Although she was nearly my height, she tilted her head back and closed her eyes, just like in the movies.

I hesitated for a second. Then I leaned forward and kissed her on the cheek. She turned her head, and our lips brushed and then pressed together. I tasted the lipstick and smoke again, but it was better this time; I didn't want the kiss to end.

Finally, Sarah stepped back. I almost lost my balance. She smiled at me.

"You're a good kisser, New Guy."

"You, too."

"Really? I've never kissed a boy before."

"I've never kissed a girl," I admitted.

She didn't seem surprised. "A natural, huh?"

"I've practiced on the mirror."

She held up her hand. "I use the back of my hand. I tried the mirror, but it left lip marks."

I pictured her practicing kissing on the back of her hand.

"I didn't lie about Lincoln."

"Whatever."

I knew she didn't believe me, but I let it go. "I'm going back."

"Okay." She returned her cigarettes while I waited by the door.

We stepped into the hallway. We hadn't gone ten feet when a shape appeared in the far doorway. I froze, aware of Sarah's hand on my back. The tech was half-turned, not looking.

"Back!" Sarah gasped, and we raced for the bathroom.

She took one stall, I took the other. We crouched with our feet on the seats, listening for footsteps. My heart was pounding so loud I was sure the tech could hear it from the hallway.

One of his shoes squeaked as he got closer, walking and pausing at a room, walking and pausing. I held my breath as the squeak stopped one more time. He was just outside the door.

Another squeak, and another, growing quiet as he headed for the nurses' station.

For the next half-hour we hung by the door, listening to him talk to the nurse, make another tour of the wing, visit the nurse again, and then finally head toward the exit door.

We waited to hear the sound of the door latch open, counted to sixty, and looked out. The corridor was empty. We made our move.

I couldn't sleep when I got back to bed. I felt charged up. I thought about Lincoln and why it was that he'd been given his strange powers. I thought about Sarah and wondered why I'd even bothered telling her about Lincoln. But she'd kissed me, anyway. I could still taste that kiss—flowers and smoke—as I lay there, as I finally fell asleep.

During the night I dreamed about Sarah. She'd grown sliver-thin and was standing against a chain link fence for support. She was smoking a huge black cigar, inhaling deep into her lungs. Smoke poured out of her mouth, her nose, her ears, her dark, sunken eyes.

Thirteen

Wednesday arrived. Lila came and got me for my session with the family.

"They're all here?" I asked.

She nodded.

I was surprised. Somebody must have told Buck he had to come.

When we walked into Lila's office, Lincoln jumped me, holding on like a leech. He felt good, like a big old Teddy bear. My mom managed to make enough space for herself to give me a hug. Buck sat with his arms folded across his chest. He nodded in my direction.

"Petey."

Bucky was on my lips, but I didn't let it out. I needed to start working on a ticket out of the place. "Hi, Buck." He looked surprised. And a little suspicious.

My mom sat on the couch; I sat next to her; Lincoln sat next to me. Buck stayed in his chair.

Seeing Lincoln and my mom should have

made me feel good, but something wasn't right. Shamed is what I felt. Chilly.

Lila leaned against the edge of her desk and flashed me a smile, warming me a bit. "We're taking good care of Peter," she said, "and he's taking good care of us. Do you want to tell your family what you've done for the past few days, Peter?"

I gave them the edited version of my days at Resthaven.

"This place sounds more like a Boy Scout camp than a hospital," Buck said. "When are you going to do something for the kid? He's sick."

"I'm sure he's getting good care, Buck," my mom said.

"We have to determine what Peter's needs are before we can do our best job," Lila said. "That's one of the reasons we're here today."

"Oh, so *that's* why. That one had me. I thought you folks were the experts."

"You're his family. You know him better than anyone else."

She glanced from Buck to my mom. I sat there, feeling like some kind of visitor from another planet who understood English but couldn't speak it. I couldn't explain to them that there was nothing wrong with me.

Lila turned to me. "What do you expect from your time at Resthaven, Peter?"

I shrugged. "I don't know." I really didn't.

"What can we do for you?"

"Let me go."

"Home?"

"I guess." It was an answer for Lincoln, but home didn't seem like a good option to me.

"What would you want from your family if you were home?" Lila asked me.

I didn't know the answer to that one either.

"Why aren't you asking us what *we* want from *him*?" Buck said.

I had my answer. "Maybe Buck could disappear."

Lincoln held tightly to my hand while the session went downhill from there. Buck and I chewed back and forth at each other. Lila tried to get my mom involved, but she mostly watched, when she wasn't staring blindly at the wall. I wanted to grab her and shake her and ask her where she'd gone.

"Do you think your husband is accurate in his assessment of Peter, Mrs. Champagne?"

"I don't know."

"Do you share his feelings?"

She glanced at Buck, not at me. "Not exactly."

I couldn't handle it any longer. "Not exactly? Not exactly? How about *not at all*? You know Buck's dead wrong, Mom. How could you take his side in this? How could you *lie*?"

"I'm not taking sides, Peter. I just want what's best for everybody." Her hands moved to her lap, where her fingers knotted and unknotted again.

"Especially yourself."

"That's not fair." At least she was talking now, but Lincoln was sliding lower on the couch. His eyes had grown wide.

Lila looked frustrated. "What about you, Lincoln? What do you think about Peter?"

Lincoln squeezed my hand and pushed in closer to me. "I love Peter."

Lila smiled. "How can we help him, Lincoln?"

Lincoln studied me, thinking it over. He wasn't used to being asked his opinion about such grownup stuff. "Let him come home," he said.

"You'd like that?"

Lincoln nodded. "I miss him." He squeezed my hand so hard it hurt.

"He'll be home before long, Lincoln."

Buck looked at his watch; my mom looked at the floor. They were both overjoyed to hear that news. But what did "before long" mean, anyway? A week? A month?

"You should probably be talking to Dr. Lubber before making any predictions," Buck said.

Lila turned to me and pointed toward the door. "Why don't you and Lincoln go sit on the couch, Peter. I'd like to talk to your parents."

Lincoln and I headed for the door. I sensed a storm coming, Lincoln looked nervous until we got to the waiting area. We took a seat on the couch, and his hand relaxed in mine.

"I saw the man with wings last night, Peter."

"What was he up to?"

"He didn't have his wings on. He was wearing a T-shirt. He was working at a computer."

"Where was he?"

"A room."

"What was in the room, Lincoln?"

"A big picture on the wall. A mountain with smoke coming out. A little picture on the desk. A baby."

Suddenly I remembered kissing Sarah. "Did you dream about anything else last night?"

His face reddened. "Maybe."

Buck, my mom, and Lila came out, single file, nobody talking.

We said good-bye quick, except for Lincoln. He gave me a long hug and whispered that he'd call me.

Lila and I walked back to the wing in silence. She headed down the hall; I headed to my bed.

I closed my eyes, but I was far from tired. I was too mad. I had no idea where my life was going.

I grabbed my pillow to fluff it up, and saw my book. *Hawk* was waiting for me like an old friend. I looked up to see Edward standing by the door, hands shoved in his pockets.

"Chess?" he said.

"Sure."

He returned in a minute with his board, and we sat on the bed and played. I was awful at first, my mind far away. But gradually I got my thoughts on the game.

"You're learning quick. But you won't get a chance to beat me after Friday."

"You're leaving Resthaven?"

"It'd be a long commute from Oakland."

"California?"

"Uh-huh. The Golden State. The land of opportunity."

"Why are you moving?"

Edward got this familiar look on his face—kind of secretive. Kind of dreamy. "New job." He chuckled. "You know that story I told you, Peter?"

"The one about you finding yourself? About you and the tent meeting?"

"And Sister Moses. Sister Moses' home church is in Oakland." His smile broadened.

"That's the reason you're moving there?"

"Mostly. But I've got a job there. And relations."

"She knows you're coming?"

"Not exactly, but I called her and she remembered me. Can you believe it? Said she'd like to see me again. So I'm going to surprise her. Sometimes you have to act on faith."

"She's not married or anything?" I was smart

121

enough to know he was interested in more than just a prayer meeting.

"Widow lady." He smiled again.

"How did you find her?"

"The relations."

I was glad for him, but not for myself. Edward was the person at Resthaven I felt most relaxed around. Everyone else was too busy for small talk and chess.

"Oakland's pretty far from here," I said.

"It's a big decision. But my daddy always said, 'Big things come of big decisions.' "

"I never knew my dad. At least, I don't remember him."

I picked up *Hawk*, pressed the crumpled bookplate over the inscription, and showed the book to Edward. "Until two nights ago, I believed what this bookplate said."

" 'To Peter, on your second birthday, Love Mom,' " Edward read.

I lifted the label and let him read what was written under it. "My mom told me that my dad died *before* I was two."

"Before?"

I nodded. "Why would she say that? Why would the inscription say something else? Why would she cover it up?"

Edward shook his head. "You think it's important?"

I wasn't sure. But if it wasn't important, why did I have this feeling gnawing at my insides? "If he wasn't dead when I was two, maybe he isn't dead now."

I figured Edward would laugh, but he just looked at me, thoughtful and unsmiling. "You're in an unhappy spot right now, but you can't fool yourself into believing your dad's going to turn up and save you from all your troubles."

"You found Sister Moses."

"Nobody ever told me she was dead."

I shrugged. "I guess I just don't trust my mom much."

"Why don't you ask her?"

"Yeah, right. You think she'd tell me anything now?"

"You can check records, newspapers. You folks are from Corpus Christi originally?"

"Yeah."

"Just get her to tell you the date your daddy died. I'll check it out for you. I can call down there to the newspaper, maybe even pull up something on the Internet."

"I'll talk to her tonight."

"Good."

Before I could call my mom, I had to sit through Group and dinner and Community. When I finally got a hold of her, it was Rec time. She seemed kind of glad to hear from me, but a little on edge.

"It was good seeing you today, Peter." She sounded like she meant it; she sounded like Buck wasn't in the room.

"You, too, Mom."

"I think we're making progress."

Now I *knew* Buck wasn't in the room. But who was it that was making progress? I figured she didn't have a clue. "How old, exactly, was I when my dad died?"

I waited for an answer. "Why?" she said finally.

"Just curious. It came up during one of my sessions. I think you told me once that I wasn't quite two."

"Yes. It was a September storm. You turned two the following January."

"Uh . . . I guess that's why I don't remember him. Because I was so young."

"Yes."

"His last name was the same as mine?

She hesitated again. "Yes. Larson. Eric Larson. I think we've talked about that, Peter."

"We were living in Corpus Christi then?"

"That's right."

"My dad was, too?"

"Uh-huh."

"What day did he die?"

"They don't know for sure," she said. "The storm came through on September tenth. Why all the questions now?"

"Lila told me to talk about it, to ask you about my dad. She thought it would help me."

"Sometimes it's better just to get on with your life, Peter."

"Did they find his boat? After the storm?"

She let out her breath with a hiss, the way she did when she was driving and got into some slow traffic. I knew she was losing her patience with me.

"No trace."

"What did he look like?"

"Peter, I—"

"Did he look like me?"

"A little. Thin. Dark hair. Your complexion."

I decided I'd pushed her far enough. "Thanks for talking to me about it, Mom." I hoped my voice sounded calm; inside I was battling my own storm.

"Hope it helps," she said half-heartedly.

I almost said good-bye. But the knot in my stomach tightened at the thought of hanging up.

"Mom?"

"Yes, Peter."

"The bookplate in *Hawk Ripley* says, 'To Peter on your second birthday, Love Mom.' "

"Eleven years," she said. "Hard to believe."

"The bookplate came off when I was reading. Underneath there's another inscription: 'Happy second birthday, Peter. May all your trails be happy. We love you. Dad and Mom.' "

I got silence. I thought for a few seconds she'd walked away from the phone. Finally her voice came back, shaky: "What are you asking, Peter?"

"Why two inscriptions? Why was one from my

dad on my second birthday when he wasn't even alive?"

Silence again, then a deep breath. "Whose writing is it, Peter?"

I pictured the handwriting. All the same—all hers. "Yours, I think."

"Right," she said, her voice calmer. "Old habits die hard. Your dad wasn't around much. I got used to signing for both of us. I remember writing in your book, then realizing what I was writing. Your dad wasn't just not around, he was never going to be around."

The spark of hope in my mind flickered and nearly went out. It was an explanation I should have thought of myself. It was obvious, logical. "So you just hid the first message with the bookplate?"

"Yes."

"Why did it matter? Did you hate him by then?"

"I didn't hate him. But he was gone. We had to get used to the idea."

She'd covered all her bases. I couldn't think of anything else to ask her. We said good-bye.

Fourteen

I lay in bed that night with the lights on, staring at the ceiling. I could feel Eugene's eyes on me as he waited for the next installment of *Hawk Ripley*, but I wasn't ready to read. I tried telling myself to believe what my mom had told me, to give up on my little-kid idea. But I couldn't do it.

I carried the book to Eugene's bed. I showed him the bookplate. "Look at this, Eugene."

He took it from me, nodded, and gave it back.

I showed him the inside cover of the book. "Now look at this."

He stared at the original note and frowned.

"My mom told me that my dad died *before* I turned two. There's no one else in my life who can tell me why she's lying, or mistaken, or if she really did just write the wrong thing to begin with."

Eugene sat silently for a minute. Then he spoke.

A lie for certain,
A bewitching weed,
Lurking in plain sight,
Posing as a forget-me-not.
But the roots—how deep?
How sour is the dirt that feeds them?

He smiled a half-sad smile.
"So you think maybe this means something?"
He nodded. I took a deep breath. At least now
there were two of us—me and the kid everyone else
thought was crazy.

Eugene glanced at the book, and I knew what
he wanted. I sat next to him and read for a while.
My mind wasn't into it, but Hawk was doing his
thing, anyway. I got to within two chapters of the
end. Exhausted, I turned off the lights and got in
bed. Even with my brain stuffed with thoughts, I
fell asleep as soon as my head hit the pillow.

❊

My sleep didn't last long. Sarah came, and we
snuck off to the girls' bathroom again. My body
was almost getting used to it. Almost.

"We *could* talk during the day," I said.

She held up her lit cigarette. "Not here. Not by ourselves. And you've been busy. Your mind's been in the clouds, New Guy."

"They're trying to figure out what's wrong with me. It's taking them some time to come up with something believable."

"They already have." She smiled, real secretive.

"Who have you been talking to?" I said.

"You don't look like a murderer, New Guy."

"A murderer?"

She pulled a scrap of paper from her shorts. "ADHD with major depression and sibling resentment resulting in homicidal ideation."

I got a sudden chill. It didn't sound like something she'd made up. *Homicidal ideation?* I figured out what it meant, but where had it come from? I grabbed the paper and looked at it: Sarah's writing, bold and angular.

"I had to write it down so I'd remember. Lubber's my doctor, too."

"He showed you my file?"

"No. He goes into his inner office to take phone calls sometimes. He thinks it's more private, but I can hear him through the door. He leaves everyone's files just sitting there, stacked on a table by his desk. I couldn't resist. I looked at mine a long time ago, then the Poet's. Now yours."

"They're *my* records."

"I thought you'd want to know."

"Did they say anything else about me?"

"Like what?"

"Something about my family. My parents. My background. Anything."

"I didn't look at everything. Why?"

I told her about the book, the bookplate, and what my mom had told me.

"What are you gonna do?" she whispered.

"I don't know. Edward said he might help me. You think it means something?"

"Eugene's smarter than you and me put together. Have you asked him?"

"He thinks it means something."

"Ask Scorpio to help you, then. What have you got to lose?"

Maybe I *did* have something to lose. Why else would my guts be knotted up like wet rope?

Fifteen

By the time I got to Lila's office the next day, I was finding it hard to focus on any one thing.

"Sit down, Peter." Lila paged through my file while I stared out her window.

"Anything new?" I said finally. My patience was paper-thin.

"I see some new *words* in here, but there's nothing new, really."

She studied my face. "Are you taking your medication now, Peter?"

I still hadn't. I almost lied, but something in the way she asked made me think she wasn't trying to nail me. "A couple of aspirin last week."

"How long has it been?"

"A long time."

"Have you noticed a difference?"

"I'm not as tired now. I feel like myself again. No dry mouth, no—"

"No restlessness? No anger? No sadness?"

"This place makes me a little sad."

"Peter, have you ever said anything about wishing you were dead?"

She seemed to be trying to lead me somewhere, but I was having a hard time following. Then the light came on. "We had kind of a fight once—my mom, Buck, and me. I said sometimes I wished I would've been on my dad's boat with him when it went down."

She nodded.

"They told you I was thinking about suicide?"

"Parents worry. Sometimes they exaggerate."

"Or lie. I was mad. They knew I didn't mean it."

"That was it? That one time?"

"I've thought a lot of times about being with my dad, but I never wanted to die. And that was the only time I ever said anything like that."

She opened my file, penned in some words. "You're doing well with your studies, you get along with the other kids, the staff. How about Dr. Lubber?"

"He thinks I'm a killer."

She looked surprised. "Why do you say that?"

"Isn't that what it says there?"

"Has Dr. Lubber been discussing your file with you?"

"No."

"Who, then?"

Now what? I couldn't snitch on Sarah. "Lubber left my file open on his desk once when he went into his other room. I peeked."

"Do you think you're a killer, Peter?" Lila asked.

For some reason I thought of Blaine Corbett. I couldn't stand him, but smashing him in the face was as far as I'd ever go. Me, a killer? I had to laugh. I don't know why, exactly, but I had to laugh. But the thought of somebody else thinking I could kill anyone, especially Lincoln, wasn't funny. I stopped laughing. "What do you think?"

"I see some anger, some distrust of what people are trying to do for you. You've got a hefty stubborn streak. Along with all your strengths, I think you have some problems, Peter. But being a killer isn't one of them. You could use some help, but not necessarily here."

I wasn't quite ready to believe what she was saying. "Jail, then?"

"Home."

Home. It felt good to hear her say it. But how good would home be? What would have changed there? Would what I'd just discovered make it worse?

"I could go home?"

"Probably not right away. There are other people involved, other opinions. It may take awhile to get everything resolved."

I guessed who the other people would be: my mom, Buck, Lubber.

"Have you seen Edward today?"

"He's here. His last day is tomorrow."

"I know."

"Looking for a chess game?"

"Yeah."

Lila took me back to the wing, where we found Edward.

"This guy wants a crack at beating you before you leave, Scorpio."

Edward laughed. "He's getting close," he lied.

We went to my room and set up the board and pieces. But I wasn't thinking much about chess. Before the first move I started talking, telling him what my mom had said.

"A big storm—a hurricane, maybe?" he said. "At least one man missing, presumed drowned, in a fishing boat accident? That shouldn't be too hard to check out. I'll make some calls."

We played one game. I did okay, considering my wandering mind. Then Edward went to make his phone calls.

A few minutes later he came back. "I left a couple of messages, but now you've got a call."

I followed him to the phone. It was Lincoln.

"The man with wings is a dad."

"How do you know that, Lincoln?"

"I saw him. I saw his little girl and his wife."

Why was Lincoln still having dreams about somebody he didn't know? And now he'd decided the man with wings was a dad? Why was that important?

Slowly at first, and then in a giant rush, something—an unstoppable current of electric hope—rose up out of my heart and poured into my brain. "What's he look like, Lincoln?"

"The dad?"

"The dad. Does he look like me?"

Lincoln laughed. "You're not a dad, Peter."

"If he was younger. If I was older. Does his face look like mine?"

I could almost hear him thinking. "He has a baseball hat on."

"What about his face?"

"Maybe. I don't know. He's old, like Mom."

Not too old. "What did his hat look like, Lincoln? What did it say on it—the letters?"

"It said S."

Big help. "Where were they, Lincoln? Inside? Outside? City? Country?"

"I could see a city. Tall buildings. Blue water. A big white boat. They were on a boat going toward the big buildings."

I heard somebody say something. "I have to go," Lincoln said into the phone.

"What else, Lincoln? What else did you see? What kind of buildings?"

There was a pause on the other end. "One was a flying saucer with long legs." Then: "Good-bye."

He hung up.

Sixteen

A flying saucer with long legs; an S. It didn't make sense. But for some reason I pictured my trading cards, and suddenly *it did*.

Edward, standing a few steps away, had heard half of my conversation with Lincoln. He looked at me, a question in his eyes. Cat glanced up from her desk.

"I'm ready to go back to my room, Edward."

Halfway down the hallway we were alone, the other kids still in the middle of their sessions.

"You ever been to Seattle?" I asked Edward.

"Seattle? Once. Years ago. Gray skies in every direction. But when the sun came out, the city sparkled like a king's treasure."

"There's a building there that looks like a flying saucer on stilts, right? I've seen it on a Sonics card."

"The Space Needle. It's part of the Sonics logo."

The Space Needle. That was what Lincoln had seen.

We got to my room. "Why Seattle?" Edward asked. "Your little brother know somebody there?"

"I don't think so. But I might." I told him what Lincoln had dreamed, how he'd dreamed other things. When I'd finished, Edward stood and stared at me, his arms folded across his chest.

"Wishful thinking, I'd call it."

I didn't feel like arguing. If he was going to ignore everything, what more could I say? "Will you still check on that other stuff for me?"

"I'm just waiting for the phone calls."

The Group sessions ended, and I went swimming with the rest of the kids. I hung on the edge of the pool and told Sarah about Lincoln's dream. She looked at me the same way she had last time, the same way Edward had.

"I'll call Lincoln up. You can talk to him if you don't believe me."

"When?"

"When we go back in. Before supper."

"You're on."

Sarah and I got permission to go to the phone together. My mom answered, but she seemed distracted and eager to let me talk to Lincoln.

"Hi, Peter."

"Hi, Lincoln." Sarah edged closer to me, and I tilted the phone away from my ear to give her a chance to listen.

"Can anybody hear you, Lincoln?"

"Mom's upstairs. Dad's out."

"Did you dream about me last night, Lincoln?"

"Yes."

I eased the air out of my lungs. "The girl you saw me with before—Sarah—was she in your dream?"

"Yes."

"She's standing here right now, Lincoln. I'm going to put her on the phone. I want you to tell her what you saw."

"Okay."

I gave Sarah the phone.

"Hi, Lincoln. I saw you on TV last night. Very handsome. What do *I* look like, Lincoln?"

She mouthed "pretty" and smiled, then "skinny" with a frown. "I don't *want* to eat more," she said a moment later. Then, "I'm not *that* skinny." Maybe Lincoln had called her a skeleton.

"Never mind. You dreamed about us last night?

Where were we?" A pause. "I asked him to come in there with me. It was okay."

Another pause. "I *like* smoking. I'll quit when I feel like it." I heard irritation in her voice, but something else, too, the same thing I saw on her face: amazement.

"What did we do then, Lincoln?"

She listened, her dark eyes widening. "What book were we talking about?"

More listening. "You told him," she whispered to me, her hand over the phone. I just smiled. I could tell by her face she didn't believe that.

"What happened then, Lincoln?"

The beginnings of a smile lit up her face. "What's yucky about it? You kiss your mom, don't you?"

Sarah's smile broadened. She leaned up against the peach-colored wall and looked at me. "No, we're too young to get married."

I reached for the phone. "Thanks, Lincoln," I said.

"Are you too young to get married, Peter?" he asked.

"Way too young. I'll talk to you later, okay?" I

hung up, and Cat took us back to the community room. We sat, pretending to watch TV.

"I believe you," Sarah said after a while.

"Good. Now what do I do?"

"Find out if your dad really lives in Seattle. Maybe he's just visiting there."

"How do I find out?"

"Call Information, I guess. But what if your mom changed your name or something?"

"She says I have his name."

She thought for a minute. "Your file. There's probably medical stuff in it—old records. There is in mine, anyway. I saw them."

I felt weird. I wasn't comfortable with the idea of being somebody besides Peter Larson.

Sarah glanced up at the wall clock. "When Lubber's not here the files are at the nurses' station. Cat goes to supper in a half-hour. Nobody's there while she's gone except for the tech going by every once in a while."

"Edward?"

"He's on duty right now."

"I don't know if he'd do it."

"Ask him."

A few minutes later he poked his head in the door and waved Sarah and me over to him.

"I've got some good news," he said. "Follow me." He led us away from the nurses' station and down the hall.

"My buddy—the one I called—is a real bull-dog once you give him a bone. That's why he took awhile getting back to me. I gave him your story and he went to every source he could think of to try to come up with some information." Edward paused long enough to cause me to stop breathing.

"And?"

"No storm," he said. "No missing fishermen. No Larson in the obituaries."

I took a deep breath and felt like I was sucking in some strange, sweet perfume.

"He checked the date your mom gave you and all around it, earlier and later," said Edward.

"What if the name wasn't Larson, Scorpio?" Sarah said.

"Then the obits wouldn't matter. But you still got no storm, no boats going down. What makes you think the name would be different?"

"My mom lied about the storm and the drowning and maybe a lot more. Why would she keep our name the same?"

Edward thought for a minute. "If she was trying to hide you from someone, she wouldn't."

"My medical records might show my real name," I said.

"Can you sneak a look for him, Scorpio?" Sarah asked.

"Cat goes to supper in a little bit," I added.

Edward glanced down the corridor toward the nurses' station, absentmindedly tapping the small bulge in his pants pocket that held his counter. "Sounds like something I could do. I'm on my way tomorrow, anyway."

"Thanks," I said.

"You two need to get back. I'll let you know what I find."

He walked us back to the community room. Sarah sat on the couch and opened a magazine. Eugene looked up from his work as I sat down in a nearby chair. My legs felt energized, ready to do some major league pacing, and I practically had to force myself to stay sitting.

"You ready for the final installment of *Hawk* tonight, Eugene?"

He nodded slightly and smiled, but his eyes looked sad. He began reciting.

Paper heroes, paper hearts,
Stir our dreams, give us hope
For gentle champions of flesh and blood,
But they touch us and they're gone.

He went back to his writing while I thought about his poem. The paper heroes part was easy, but who were the flesh-and-blood champions? Edward, with one day to go until he was gone? Or could Eugene be talking about me? Had he somehow figured out that I wouldn't be around much longer?

Edward came to the door and casually looked around the room. Then he turned and left. I followed him. Sarah was nowhere in sight.

"I went through your whole file, Peter—everything I thought might be helpful, anyway. Two things jumped out at me."

A heavy, watery feeling seeped into my chest.

"First, Lubber's got a problem. He's way off base with you."

It was nice to hear Edward say it, but Lubber's problem wasn't exactly news to me.

"Almost wasn't a number two. I was about ready to clear out of there when I came across something stuck in the back of your folder." He took a piece of paper from his hip pocket and handed it to me. "It's a copy of a copy, but it's readable."

The paper was a printed form with hand-written notes scribbled here and there. Everything was a little out of focus. It was a record of a physical exam.

There were entries for immunizations, respiration, pulse, blood pressure, height, and weight. Thirty-one inches, twenty-six pounds. A baby. I looked for the date of birth and found it on top of the page, typed, lost in all the print: my birthday. Above it another date was typed in: I'd just turned one.

My eyes raced up and down and back and forth across the form, looking for a name, and I found it in the upper right-hand corner, written sideways on the page, faded, nearly cut off: my name, but not my name. Peter, yes. James, yes. *Nordquist.*

I looked at Edward, who stuck out his hand. "Good to meet you, Mr. Nordquist."

I took his hand and shook it, feeling nothing. "She lied."

"It doesn't mean your dad's alive."

"I know. But it means he could be. Can we call Seattle and ask if there's a Nordquist?"

"Based on what—your little brother's dream?"

"Lincoln's dream was real. And remember when you asked me where I was from? You said I sounded not quite Texas."

"Not quite Texas doesn't necessarily mean Seattle. And every little kid thinks their dreams are real."

"Lincoln's are. Ask Sarah."

"I'll do that, Peter. But right now I've got stuff to do: work stuff, leaving-town stuff. You need to talk to someone you trust—Lila, maybe—about what's going on. Let me know what happens."

He headed down the hall. I waited for the click of his counter. "I know how you can get credit for a whole bunch of good deeds in a hurry," I said to his back.

He stopped and stared at me.

"Take me with you. Seattle and Oakland—they're pretty close. You could just drop me off on your way." I pictured the U.S. map tacked to my bedroom wall. It was only a few inches between northern California and Washington.

"A thousand miles apart. Not on the way to anywhere."

"Eight hundred, maybe. A day's drive."

Edward walked back to me, glancing around at the empty corridor. "You know what kind of trouble I'd get in, taking you across country for any reason?" he whispered. I could hear my heart begging for him to say yes. "Much less on a wild goose chase to look for a father who probably isn't alive, in a place you decided on because your baby brother dreamed about it?"

The idea *did* sound stupid. And he *could* get in a lot of trouble. "I guess I'll talk to Lila."

"Do that." He started down the hall again. He was halfway to the emergency exit before I heard the click.

Seventeen

Cat wasn't back at the nurses' station yet, and no one else was around. I looked in the phone book and punched in the Seattle area code and Information number using my mom's calling card.

"Seattle," I said to the recording. "Nordquist." A live operator came on. "I'm not sure of the first name," I said.

"Checking." Her flat voice was followed by a flatter silence. "I show two: an A. Nordquist on Nineteenth Northwest and a James Nordquist, on North Sixty-sixth."

James. My middle name. I asked for both numbers and dialed A. Nordquist's first.

An old lady answered. In a loud voice she told me that she didn't know anyone named Peter and never had. She didn't know James Nordquist, either.

I called the other number and waited. The

phone stopped ringing. My throat felt so tight, I didn't know if I'd be able to talk.

A man's voice came on—a recording, cheerful and friendly: "You've reached the Nordquist residence, but Laura and I are off to the wild blue yonder, and Missie's at Grandma's house until August twelfth. If you'll leave an interesting message after the beep, we'll be sure to call you back."

I heard the beep and stood there like a department-store dummy. Did the voice sound familiar? I tried to tell myself yes, but I was lying. It was no more familiar than the old lady's, or the man in the moon's.

I had an interesting message, but I had no idea how to say it. I hung up the phone and sank to the floor. What had his message said?

Gone till August twelfth. That was three more days. Not very long, but a lifetime just the same. What else? *Off to the wild blue yonder.* I knew what that meant, kind of, but it took a minute for me to make the connection: in the sky; flying; *the man with wings.*

I jumped up and ran down the hallway, looking for Edward. He must have heard me coming. He came out of Sam's room and waited for me.

"You found a Nordquist?"

I skidded to a stop, heart thumping. "In Seattle."

"Good. Now we just need to call the other thousands of cities and towns in this big country and see how many more Nordquists there are."

"I called one and got a recording. It said they'd be back in three days, that they were off to the wild blue yonder."

"Uh-huh."

"Don't you see? Lincoln's dream. The man with wings. He must be a pilot or something."

"That was a dream, Peter."

"It was *real!*" My voice must have gotten louder. Down the hall Cat walked up to the nurses' station and stopped to stare at us.

"Tell Lila. Tell Cat. They're good people. I can't take you with me."

I tried to read his eyes. I saw no belief, no sign that he was going to change his mind.

"Fine," I said at last. I headed back to the community room.

❋

Sarah thought for a minute before she said anything. "What are you gonna do?"

"I'm going to go find out. I'm going to Seattle."

She lowered her voice. "You even know how to get there?"

"The bus driver can figure it out."

"They'll track you down."

"Maybe. Maybe I'll hitchhike."

"You'll need money."

"I've got a little money. More at home. More in the bank."

"I have some money. You can have it."

"Keep it. I'll be okay."

"How soon?"

"Tonight."

She looked at me. "He'll be home in three days," she said. "You could talk to him then."

What would waiting do? I didn't want to hear James Nordquist over the phone.

"I ain't waiting."

"It'll take you at least three days to get there."

"I know."

Sarah breathed deep, took my hand, stared straight ahead. I knew I was turning red, but nobody was looking. I held on and felt the heat from her hand work its way up my arm.

"You have a plan?" she whispered, still looking away.

"Kind of."

"Need help?"

"I think so."

"You won't find a better helper than me," she said. "I know my way around this place. I know who goes where and what time they go. I can sneak around, get stuff, do anything you need me to do. Just ask."

I had to smile. I'd been wondering if I should even get her involved. "Thanks."

"You'll let me?"

"You could get in trouble."

She shrugged and squeezed my hand tighter. "I'm counting on it."

"Okay. I'm asking for your help."

"You've got it."

Eighteen

Eugene sat up in bed, waiting. I'd gathered a few things and stuffed them in a small duffel bag of Sarah's while he was in the bathroom. I sat down and opened up *Hawk*.

"You ready, Eugene?"

He nodded.

I read, saying the words but listening to my mind race through a thousand other thoughts. When the end of the story came—when Hawk had made his last rescue and put away the bad guys for good—I barely recognized it. But the words ran out. I stopped reading. Eugene's eyes were glassy, his cheeks shiny.

"You okay?"

New Guy Peter looks for roots,
Finds a friend, finds a friend.
Eugene the Poet sees him come,
Sees him go, sees him go.

Tastes the bitter and the sweet,
Something gained, something lost.

I hadn't fooled Eugene. I sat down next to him and handed him the book. "I don't like it here, Eugene. I don't think I belong here. But I've made some good friends. You're one of them."

He looked at the book.

"It's yours." I went to my bed and turned out my light. Eyes closed, heart thumping, I listened to the pages turn until I fell asleep.

When Sarah came I was on the edge of being awake, ready for her touch.

"It's time," she whispered. She stood in the shadows while I threw on a T-shirt and my shoes and socks.

"Ready, New Guy?" She stepped close and gave me a hug that took my breath away. I put my arms around her and held her for a second, feeling the ribs branching out from her bony spine, the feathery touch of her cheek, smelling the smoky perfume clinging to her hair.

She pulled away. "Take care, Peter," she said, and ghosted from the room.

I threw some clothes under the blanket on my bed and arranged them to look like feet and legs. If the tech glanced in, he would only see the bottom half of my bed. He might be fooled for a while.

I heard voices, far off at first and then louder, closer. I listened for the latching of the door, but it didn't come, and still the voices—Sarah's and the tech's—grew louder. My head was aching and my ears rang, but Sarah's voice came through as I eased back into the shadows.

"I wasn't trying to run away."

"You could've fooled me."

"I just wanted some fresh air."

"Where'd you get the cigarette?"

"Found it."

They were right outside my door. I hung back, willing my insides to calm down.

"You don't leave the building at night."

"The door was open."

"Not for you. Nurses' station. *Now.* I need to write you up."

"Great."

I listened to Sarah's voice melt away. It was filled

with pepper and vinegar as she told the tech what she thought of him.

Something grabbed the leg of my shorts. I jumped, nearly dropping my bag. Eugene was there, sitting up in the dark. "Sorry, Peter," he whispered.

"You okay, Eugene?" I could still hear Sarah's voice, but it was faint, the sound of a bubbling pot. They had to be nearly to the nurses' station.

"I'm fine. Are you leaving now?"

"In about two seconds," I said, and suddenly it hit me: Eugene was talking like a regular person. It was weird, me having to leave just as this was happening. I didn't know what to say.

"How?" he said.

"Emergency exit. Sarah's helping."

"Good luck." We shook hands.

I took a step toward the door. "Take care of Sarah, Eugene. Make her eat."

"Like a lumberjack," he said, and then held up *Hawk*. "Thanks for this." That was it. Just *Thanks for this.* No more lines, no rhymes. He took a breath that sounded more like a sob.

"You're gonna be fine, Eugene."

I couldn't wait any longer. I went to the door and peeked out. At the nurses' station, the tech stood with his back to me, facing Sarah. Sarah's voice grew louder. I knew she'd seen me.

I gave her a quick wave and took off, giant-stepping down the hall. I shouldered along the wall. Doorways floated by me as I rushed toward the big black opening at the end of the corridor. I waited for a shout, for someone to call my name.

It didn't happen, and I flew out of the building like the devil was on my tail. I ran and stumbled in the warm, sticky darkness, heading toward the empty street.

I reached the sidewalk and cut left, sprinting past shade trees, through dim circles of light filtering down from lonely street lamps. My legs felt tight, my chest ached. Somewhere up ahead was the highway.

Half a block away, headlights flashed out from a cross street and bent in my direction. I ducked into a driveway and backed against a leafy hedge. Five seconds—a lifetime—later, a cop car cruised past, purring like a tiger. Sweating, dry-mouthed, I waited until I was sure it was gone.

Then I sprinted up the street.

I made it to the main road without seeing another person. A few blocks away, the red sign of a cafe lit up the dusty dark. A couple of cars and a truck sat out front. I studied the cafe from the shadows of its parking lot. Open 24 Hours, the sign said, and inside a waitress wandered between three booths, where three men sat by themselves eating. I decided to wait for one of them to come out. I didn't care for the idea of standing on the side of the road like a human billboard and trying to hitchhike. Not unless I had to.

In a few minutes a man got up, paid at the cash register, and walked out, poking a toothpick at his teeth. By the time he got to his car I was standing by it, screwing up my courage. He stopped a few feet away and eyed me like he would a stray dog. I had to fight off the urge to run.

"Shouldn't you be home in bed, son?" He spit a chunk of toothpick.

"You going to Deadwood?"

He studied me for a few seconds. "Harding. Opposite direction. Sorry."

He got in and drove off, glancing in his rearview

mirror. I watched him, trying to see if he was going to pick up a cell phone and make a call.

A semi rig—going the right way—pulled in. The driver got out, checked his tires, and walked into the cafe. He sat down at the counter and opened a menu. It would be awhile before he'd be back.

More time passed. I pictured myself spending all night in the cafe parking lot, begging for rides. I'd almost decided to take my chances thumbing it when the next guy got up and headed for the door. He was thin and white-haired and old—seventy, maybe. I had no trouble getting to his pickup before he did.

"Don't get too close to that vehicle, little buddy. My alarm system might go off."

I heard a low growl behind me and half-jumped, half-staggered away from the truck. His alarm system—a big-toothed, black-and-white sheepdog—had gotten up from its nap and was standing in the bed of the pickup, giving me the evil eye.

"Good girl, Sydney." The man scratched the dog around the scruff of her neck and slipped his big hand under her collar. I figured if he said the word, Sydney would be on me in a flash.

I started to ease away. The side of the highway was looking better all the time.

"Can I do something for you, little buddy?" His smile was full of too-white, too-even teeth, and I tried to read it. Friendly? Phony? Friendly, I decided.

"I need a ride to Deadwood." I had an excuse ready—I'd been visiting a friend and missed the last bus home—but he didn't ask for an excuse.

"I'm goin' that way. Hop in."

I climbed up on the seat while the old guy held the door open. He clapped his hands, and Sydney leaped to the pavement. "Cab," he said, and suddenly she was in the cab with me, making herself a space on the floor, sniffing me up and down.

"Name's Les," he said as we pulled out of the parking lot.

"Good to meet you." I waited for him to ask my name—John, I would've said—but he didn't. We rolled down the mostly empty highway, mostly not talking. The radio was tuned to a country music station, and every once in a while Les would talk over it, mostly about Sydney, who had decided that I was okay. She spent half the trip licking the sweat off my legs while I petted her and thought about my old dog, Cowboy.

Les dropped me off a couple of blocks from my house. Buck's big car sat empty in our driveway, and the house stood black and silent behind its windows. I relaxed a little. No one from Resthaven had called. Yet.

The door was locked. I soft-shoed it to the backyard and looked up at my bedroom window: closed tight. Lincoln's was my last good hope. And it was open. Wide open.

I knew the combination to the padlock on the shed door. I found the aluminum ladder by touch, carefully hauled it out, and leaned it gently against the house.

Lincoln was lying on his side with his back to me when I slipped through his window. I stood next to his bed for a minute, listening to him breathe. Then I crept down the hall. Half of me was tuned to my insides, which felt like someone had twisted them up like spaghetti on a fork. The other half was focused on the empty silence of the house, waiting for the ring of the phone to fill it. Then what would I have done?

I had a built-in map in my head that let me find my way around my room in the purest dark. I went to my desk, bottom drawer, left side. My mouth was dry, and I swallowed hard as I slid out the drawer. I found the old cigar box right where I'd left it—in the back, behind the two thick binders full of baseball and basketball cards.

The coins in the box would make a fearsome noise if I dropped it. But I got it to the rug and lifted the lid. Inside were the coins—half a box full—and the envelope where I kept the folding money, but right away I knew something was wrong. The envelope was too light.

Nearly three hundred dollars—most of my allowance for the past year plus whatever I'd made mowing lawns and selling sports cards—was gone.

My mind spun into gear. What next? I remembered my mom telling me to get the money to the bank. She knew it was in the drawer. Buck must have known. What about Lincoln?

"I didn't take it, Peter." The voice was a whisper, but it nearly knocked me over. I jumped up and saw Lincoln halfway into the room. He came to me, gave me a hug, and held on.

"What are you doing up, Lincoln?" I whispered.

"I saw you. I saw you in your room. In my dream."

I moved him to arm's length so I could see his face. "Who took the money, Lincoln? Where is it?"

He shrugged. "Dad, maybe. Mom, maybe. Not me."

"I know not you." I stood there, trying to think. I still had some money in my bank account. Maybe it was *all* there now. I had to get to the bank.

"I want to go with you, Peter." I noticed for the first time that he was wearing his street clothes. "I know you're going somewhere."

"You can't go, Lincoln."

"I *want* to."

I actually considered it for a few seconds. Lincoln would be the one person I'd miss.

"No way, Lincoln. You need to go back to bed. You need to forget I was ever here."

"Please, Peter?" His whisper had gotten louder. I tried to put my hand over his mouth, but he pulled away. "I'd be good."

"You'd be a giant weight on my shoulders, Lincoln, a magnet for trouble."

He stood there, not saying anything for a moment. "A weight?" He wiped at his eye.

"A big one. Big trouble."

I walked him back to his room, tucked him in, and gave him a hug. I glanced at the clock: 3:30. For just a moment I thought about looking in on my mom, seeing her face one more time, collecting a picture for my mind. But I had better memories of her. And it would be too dangerous to open her bedroom door.

I crawled through the window, figuring I had nearly six hours to kill before the bank opened. I needed a place to hide.

Nineteen

The bank was only about a mile from our house. But my legs were heavy and twitchy, and I had that empty, sick feeling in my stomach that comes with no sleep. I didn't take the direct route; I stuck with back streets and dark sidewalks until I came to a low bridge that passed over a dry creek bed. Just before the bridge rail started, a dirt trail veered off down the grass embankment. I took it, knowing what was down there: a big drainpipe that cut a hole through the dirt and under the bridge.

The entrance to the pipe was a darker circle against the dark ground that held it. Its size was just right if I ducked down a bit, but I wasn't ready to go inside that inky tunnel.

Snakes and skunks and spiders and scorpions crept and crawled through my mind as I pitched a golf-ball-sized rock into the hole. The sound of rock against dirty cement was followed by silence. Then a light scurrying sound. Rats?

I bowled a bigger rock into the entrance. This time the sound was louder—distant thunder—but there were no after-sounds. I went in about three steps. Not far, but far enough to be out of sight. And close enough to get out in a hurry if I had to. I squatted down with my back against the curve of the pipe, put my bag under my head, and stretched out as well as I could.

The dirt was dry under me, but I was sweating in the sticky air. I closed my eyes and listened to the outside sounds—crickets, a car passing overhead, a radio somewhere off in the distance. I listened for sounds from inside the pipe: nothing. Finally I faded off to sleep.

❊

Sunlight, bright and hot, was beating its way into the pipe by the time I woke up. I glanced at my watch: 9:20. The bank would be open. And they'd be awake at Resthaven, knowing by now that I was gone. My mom and Buck would know, too.

I half-stood, feeling stiff and dry-mouthed and tired and empty, except for a bladder that was about to burst. I relieved myself on the dirt. Then I brushed myself off and slipped from the pipe.

I waited for a car to pass by overhead and scrambled up the bank to the street. No one was in sight. At Fellows Street I took a right, walking past stores and businesses. More cars passed. I tried not to look, sure as anything that I'd hear the screech of brakes and have to take off running.

But nobody stopped. People on the sidewalk didn't pay me any mind. And finally I stood in front of the bank.

I ducked through the door, putting on my best smile, enjoying the air-conditioned cool of the big room. I felt like a bank robber.

As I filled out a withdrawal slip, I looked around: two other customers, one in line, one at the teller's window; a man and a woman at desks over to the side. I was pretty sure none of them knew me. I finished writing and got in line.

The guy in front of me was wearing gray coveralls that said Kelsey's Coffee Service on the back. He set a big zippered bag on the counter and pulled out a wad of checks and green money. This was going to take too long. What if someone who knew me walked in?

Finally the teller finished her counting and computer work and gave the guy a receipt and a smile.

She turned it down a notch for me, but it was still friendly as I handed her the withdrawal slip.

She looked at the paper. "How are you today, Mr. Larson?" Her voice seemed loud above the dull sounds of the bank.

"Fine. How are you?" I tried to sound casual, like I did this every day.

"Do you have some picture ID?"

"No." Her smile faded some more. "I'm only thirteen." My empty stomach didn't like the direction the conversation was heading.

"We require picture ID for amounts over two hundred dollars."

Two hundred dollars? I was going for $550— about what I figured I had in the account.

"We'll have to limit the withdrawal to two hundred. Or you can ask the custodial account holder to come in with you."

"My mother?"

She punched in some stuff on her computer. "Sandra Champagne." She looked at me blankly, hoping, I guessed, that I'd decide what to do, or maybe just go away.

"How about I take the two hundred, walk out the door, come back in, get the next two hundred, and so on?"

"It's two hundred per *day*." Her smile was gone.

The man who had been at the desk was up now, moving in next to her. He was big and wide and took up most of the space in her tiny cubicle. "Do we have a problem here, Cindy?"

She showed him the withdrawal slip. "He has no ID."

"Did Cindy explain our policy, son?"

I nodded. He glanced at the slip again and then looked at me for what seemed like forever. "This your signature here?"

"Yes."

"Need that money pretty badly?"

How was I supposed to answer that? "I'd like to have it. It's mine."

He studied me again. "I'll tell you what I'm gonna do. We should have a signature card on file for you. I'm gonna take a look."

The big man moved back to a row of file

cabinets and began slowly scanning their labels. Finally he pulled open a drawer. I looked up at the wall clock. It was nearly ten.

The man fingered his way through the drawer front to back, as if there were no filing system. He closed the drawer empty-handed and opened another. My heartbeat picked up a notch. He turned and smiled at me and for a second seemed to look past me, toward the door. I glanced behind me. Nothing.

I waited, wondering when the next bus heading west would be leaving town.

Street sounds got louder behind me, and I knew someone else had walked through the door. The big man looked, straightened up, and turned away from the cabinet. He gazed past me with a kind of twitchy smile. "You were quick."

I turned. Buck stood there, not six feet away, blocking the way out. "Goin' somewhere, Petey?"

I thought about making a run for it. But Buck was close enough to reach out and grab me, and his sidekick was now standing a few feet away with his big body ready to spring. I wouldn't have stood a chance.

"I guess not, Bucky."

Buck gave me a look and nodded to his buddy.

"Appreciate it, Billy."

Billy nodded back.

"Judas," I said, and Billy's smile faded.

"You got trouble there, Buck."

"Nothing I can't handle."

Buck wrapped his big hand around my bicep and steered me through the door and into the front seat of his idling car. He slammed my door and started around to the driver's side.

Lincoln was sitting in the back. "I didn't tell, Peter."

"I know you didn't, Lincoln. It wasn't your fault."

Buck had swung open his door by the time I made my decision. *You always have a choice,* Lila had told me. I pulled the ignition key and scrambled out my side.

I tripped and sprawled on my hands and knees. I jumped to my feet, but Buck was heading toward me, slow and certain.

"The keys, Petey. And get in the car."

I ran along the front of the bank, but Buck

stayed between me and the street and closed in on me again. I turned and took off down the alley, eyeing a big wooden gate at the end. It had to be open.

It wasn't. I pulled on the handle and the gate rattled back at me like dry bones. I dropped my bag and tried jumping high enough to grab onto the top, but I couldn't.

When I turned, Buck was halfway down the alley, taking his time.

"Give it up, boy. You and the keys. Don't make me get mad."

He was already way past mad. "I'll give them to you. Just let me go."

"Your momma's waiting."

Lincoln appeared at the entrance to the alley. He held onto a big mailbox as if he was having trouble standing up. "Are you okay, Peter?"

"Get back in the car, Lincoln," Buck growled.

"Don't hurt Peter, Dad!"

"Get in the car. *Now.*" Buck turned back to me, slowly moving in for the kill. Lincoln let go of the mailbox and took a couple of steps toward us.

Suddenly I pictured those corny TV ads and Lincoln snagging that football.

I pulled the keys from my pocket. "Catch, Lincoln!" I yelled to him.

For a second I thought he hadn't heard me. But he held up his hands in front of him, ready.

"Where's that gonna get ya, Petey? You think Lincoln can run away from me on those little round legs?"

I bent my knees and lofted the keys underhanded. They flew, arcing high over Buck's reach as they headed for Lincoln's outstretched hands. Before they got there, Buck had turned and started for the little guy like a wide receiver going out for a pass.

But Lincoln squinted, concentrating. He caught the keys cleanly with Buck bearing down on him like a landslide. I saw a little smile cross Lincoln's face.

"Mail 'em, Lincoln!" He froze, and for a second I thought for sure Buck had him. "Drop 'em in the mailbox!"

Lincoln took two quick steps and mailed the keys just as Buck got to him. They clanked on the metal floor of the box.

Buck grabbed Lincoln by the arm but then

suddenly let go, figuring, I guess, that he had bigger fish to land. I was flying toward that one little space where he wasn't. He took a step, narrowing that gap, and I figured I wasn't going to make it. He tried another step, but something stopped him.

Lincoln was clinging to Buck's leg like eighty pounds of ivy. Buck reached toward me with one arm while trying to pry Lincoln loose with the other. But he was too burdened, and I slipped past him and accelerated for the street. I got to the sidewalk and veered left.

"Thanks, big guy!" I yelled to Lincoln. Buck was shouting at him, but he wasn't letting go.

I put my head down and flew, whipping past buildings and curious faces. At the corner I looked back—no one there—then headed toward the bridge and the pipe.

I heard a car coming, and I ducked behind a garage and waited, breathing deep, chest aching. Sweat glued my T-shirt to my skin.

When I looked out, the car was gone. The street was empty in both directions. I walked for a while. I didn't see anyone. I timed my arrival at the bridge so no cars would pass while I was heading down the embankment to the creek bed.

I stumbled inside the pipe and sat, my back against the curve of the cement. I needed to make plans but all I wanted to do was nothing. I felt tired and hungry and thirsty and running on empty. And I was broke. The few dollars in my wallet wouldn't get me much past the outskirts of town.

I thought about Lincoln and what he had done for me. I wanted to make sure he was okay. But I knew he was; he was Buck's pride and joy.

I felt the sweat cool and dry on my skin. I thought about being thirsty and hungry, about the store I'd passed on the way to the bank. It would've been easy to walk the few blocks to get there. But who would be out looking for me? I decided to wait.

The day stayed quiet. I dozed off a couple of times and then fell into a deep, dark sleep. I dreamed about Resthaven mostly: Sarah, Eugene. And Edward, dressed like Hawk Ripley, riding out of a hole in the ground on a huge horse. When I woke up it was 2:20 in the afternoon, and I knew what I had to do.

Twenty

The store sat back off the street a ways, and the phone booth was tucked behind a dumpster. But I still felt naked and exposed as I punched in the number and my mom's calling card number. I sipped root beer and listened to my stomach growl, working on the hot dog I'd just downed.

A voice answered: "Good afternoon, Resthaven." Marianne.

I bunched up the bottom of my T-shirt and held it over the mouthpiece. "Edward Lang, please." I used my lowest voice, but it came out squeaky.

"Beg pardon?"

"Edward Lang." Better this time.

"I'll ring his extension."

I held my breath. Would I be able to fool anyone else?

"Residential North." Cat's voice. I almost hung up. But what did I have to lose?

"Edward Lang, please."

"Edward?" A pause. "I don't see him right now. May I have him call you?"

Call me? "I can wait."

Another pause, and I was afraid for an instant that she'd recognized my voice.

"I'll page him for you." She put me on hold. Was she really paging him, or making another phone call? I waited, both eyes on the street now. In my mind I mapped out an escape route in case Buck showed up.

The music stopped. "This is Edward."

"It's me. It's Peter."

For what seemed like forever there was nothing, then: "Russell! How you been?"

Russell? I didn't get it. But then I pictured Edward standing at the nurses' station with Cat sitting there, listening to every word.

"I'm tired. I've been on the run."

"That's great. Nothing like a vacation to recharge those batteries. So where are you now?" His voice was easy, relaxed.

I told him where I was, that I was broke, where I'd spent the night. "Will you take me to Seattle?"

"That would be great."

"It would? Really?"

"Really."

I wanted to ask him why, but I knew his half of the conversation was being shared. "When?"

"I didn't tell you, Russell, but you just got me in the *nick* of time. I'm heading west." He paused. "Yeah, that's right. California. This evening, as a matter of fact. But since it's my last day, they're taking it easy on me here at work. I'm off at six. I can stop and say good-bye on my way out of town."

"What time?"

"Let's shoot for seven-thirty."

"Where?"

"I can pick you up at the motel—the place you stayed last night. Keep your ears open. I'll honk twice."

"Thanks, Edward."

"It'll be great to see you after all this time."

He hung up. I walked as casually as I could out of the parking lot and down the street. But I felt pumped up; I felt like I was floating.

Twenty-one

The afternoon dragged by. The inside of the pipe grew hotter and I grew sleepier, but I was afraid to fall asleep.

Just after six, a big brown dog showed up at the entrance. He looked friendly, but I figured his owner would appear next. I got ready to head for the other end of the pipe. Then I heard a kid's voice calling from somewhere up above.

"Brutus!" And Brutus took off, leaving a thin cloud of dust to drift into the pipe.

Seven o'clock came, then seven-fifteen. Cars approached and hummed past, but none slowed.

Seven-thirty came and went; seven-forty-five. I imagined one bad thing after another: he couldn't find me; he'd gotten in a wreck; he'd only been try-ing to get me off the phone; he wasn't coming, but

Buck was, or the cops, or some kind of posse from Resthaven. I pictured Lubber leading the pack. Where was Hawk when I needed him?

Eight o'clock came. I started wondering what my chances would be of hitchhiking to Seattle with no money, no clothes, nothing.

A car approached and slowed, and continued across the bridge. I prayed for it to stop, but the sound of the engine gradually faded away. A minute later the sound was back, coming from the opposite direction. I heard the tires roll by overhead, then a soft squeak of brakes, then an engine idling, a horn honking. Twice.

I scrambled out of the pipe and up the bank. On the other side of the street, pulled to the side, sat a green Ford wagon, loaded with boxes.

The driver's side window, tinted smoky gray, eased down. Edward gave me a half-grin and signalled me over.

I crossed the street and jumped in, and Edward pulled slowly away from the curb. In the distance a car approached, its headlights already on in the dusk. Edward motioned me down. "Why don't you stay out of sight until we clear the city limits.

There's folks here who know you, and know you don't belong with me."

I scooted down. The car passed, then another, and Edward made some turns, picked up speed, and headed for the highway.

He stopped at a stoplight. The turn signal clicked, a clock ticking off seconds. They seemed like hours. How many reasons were there for a cop to decide to pull us over?

Finally the light changed, and Edward turned onto the highway with his big foot pressed hard against the gas pedal.

Minutes passed. The light grew dimmer. My legs were getting numb and tingly, and I shifted my weight and squirmed around.

"It's safe to sit up." Edward reached behind the seat as I snapped on my seat belt. He handed me a small cooler. "I figured you'd need this."

I popped open the top. Inside were sandwiches and candy bars, with cans of soda wedged in ice.

"Thanks." I didn't mean just for the food. I downed half a can without taking a breath.

Outside it was near dark. The land was brown and bare, with a house or ranch building here and there against the flat horizon. The only headlights were a long way off. A saxophone played slow and sad on the stereo. But I wasn't sad. I was excited. And hungry.

I bit off a mouthful of sandwich, enjoying the taste of ham and cheese. But I couldn't wait to ask my question: "Why'd you change your mind?"

"Stupidity."

"No, really. Why?"

Edward looked through the windshield for a long while, squinting at the oncoming headlights. "I had a conversation with Sarah the evening before you took off. She told me she'd talked to your little brother. She told me what he'd seen. She almost convinced me."

"Almost?"

"Not quite. But I did a lot of thinking after we found out you were gone. I thought about all the little things I'd done for people, all the safe things. I'd counted up a bunch of stuff, but none of it amounted to much. I remembered telling you that sometimes you have to act on faith. I've seen a lot of kids, and I realized how much I believed in you. I decided that faith and belief go hand in hand, that

I'd missed an opportunity to really help someone in a way that mattered.

"Then you called. You gave me another chance. I took it."

"I'm glad I tried one more time."

Edward didn't say anything for a minute, and I figured he hadn't heard me. Finally he took a long breath and let it out slow. "Me, too," he said.

We drove on. When the sky turned black, my eyelids got too heavy to keep open, and I imagined I could hear my mom humming "Sweet Hour of Prayer." Some of its hopeful words drifted to me through the fog: "Sweet hour of prayer, sweet hour of prayer/Thy wings shall my petition bear." I fell asleep thinking of the man with wings.

I woke up awhile later; we were still heading down the highway. Edward had draped a big leather jacket over me. I dozed off again.

I woke once more. This time the car wasn't moving. Edward was gone, and lights—gas station lights—were beaming in the window. The only sound was the hum of the gas pump.

The pump clicked off. Edward came out of the little store with a cup of coffee. He hung up the hose and got in. "You awake?"

I looked around. We were out in the middle of nowhere. "Kind of."

"New Mexico." He held up the coffee. "Want some?"

It smelled good, but I'd tasted coffee before. "No, thanks."

He pointed at the cooler. "Help yourself."

"Okay." But I scooted down in the seat again.

While I slept, we crossed into Arizona.

We finished the rest of the food in the cooler sometime after sunup. We made another gas stop, Edward got a bigger cup of coffee, and we kept on rolling. At Flagstaff we turned north, and I started feeling like we were getting somewhere.

Later, Edward turned up the music, turned up the air conditioner, rolled down his window, and stuck his face out in the wind like a dog.

"You tired?" I asked him.

"Getting there."

"When are you going to sleep?"

"I want to get out of Arizona first."

"It's a big state."

"Yeah. But it's not Texas."

We entered Utah. I breathed easier, but Edward kept driving. More gas, drive-through burgers. I didn't care what we ate. And the less time we took doing it, the better.

The sun was high above us when Edward pulled his counter out of his pocket and set it on the dashboard. "What's it worth, Peter?"

"What you're doing for me, you mean?"

"If I get you to Seattle, what's it worth?"

"How many do you need?"

"Seventeen. I was down to seventeen when I left Resthaven."

"You've done big stuff for me since then."

"I want to wait till we're there. All or nothing. What do you think?"

"Eighteen. At least."

"Good." He put the counter back in his pocket, turned up the music a bit, and began humming along with it. I leaned back and closed my eyes.

I woke up to the car slowing. Just another gas station. Edward started to pull into a set of pumps. A dusty red pickup sped in from the opposite direction and skidded to a stop, leaving us no room to go ahead. Edward stopped and we sat there, bumper to bumper with the pickup. Two guys stared coldly at us through their windshield. Edward stared back. He got that look I'd seen when he and Buck were squaring off back at Resthaven. My insides got tight and jumpy.

Edward put the gear shift in reverse and eased back, mumbling something under his breath. The two guys smiled and rolled forward, taking our spot. Edward turned the wheel and cut over to the other island. He got out and began filling the tank. "Back in a minute," he said through the window, and went inside.

Beyond the gas-stop pavement was red dirt and more red dirt reaching off to some hills in the distance. I got out to stretch my legs. I could see Edward standing near the counter, waiting to pay.

"Your buddy made the right decision, son."

The voice made me jump. One of the guys in the pickup was standing by the front fender of Edward's car. My side. He wore dirty white high-tops and blue jeans and nothing else but tattoos. The ones on his arms I couldn't see much of; the ones on his chest were a smiling skull and this guy who looked like the grim reaper, riding a motorcycle down from the clouds. The angel of death, I figured. Scary, but not as scary as the guy himself. He gave me the spinal willies.

I turned away. I didn't want trouble any more than Edward did, but when I looked back the guy's bloodshot eyes were still on me.

"You wanna know *why* he made the right decision, son?"

"Not really." I looked toward Edward, hoping he'd see me and hurry.

The guy stepped closer. I heard the gas pump click off, I smelled stale tobacco.

"Because my buddy's in a bad mood today. He's in a *butt-kickin'* mood. And he don't like no salt-and-pepper crap goin' on."

I didn't know what he was talking about.

"Don't you got no pride, boy? Don't you care who you're hangin' with?"

Now I got it.

Out of the corner of my eye I saw his buddy coming, walking with a cocky, side-to-side roll. He shouldered up next to his pal and gave me a look.

"You gonna answer him?" He was bigger and broader and had a smell to match. His face was round and red under a greasy yellow baseball cap.

"I *do* care." I saw Edward walk out the door; I saw his posture change as he took in the scene. "So why don't you guys get out of my face?"

It was maybe not the smartest thing to say. Tattoo took a step forward, chesting me up against the car. The rearview mirror poked me in the spine, folding me backwards. His face hung three inches from mine, and I had to swallow hard to keep from breathing him in.

"Out of your face? You want me out of your face?" His voice rose, his spit flew against my cheek, and I closed my eyes.

Suddenly he was gone. When I opened my eyes, Edward had one huge forearm under the guy's chin, dragging him away. Yellow Cap was stalking them slowly. Edward's dance partner was trying to say something, but it came out a weak gurgle.

"You best let go of him, *Midnight!*" Yellow Cap snarled, and reached toward his boot.

"Get in the car, Peter. Lock your door."

I thought about running inside and getting someone to call the cops. But there wasn't time. And I couldn't just leave.

Yellow Cap straightened up with something black in his hand. A blade flashed out, long and thin, sunlight dancing off it as he waved it high in front of him.

Edward jerked his forearm against Tattoo's throat and stepped back, letting him drop to the pavement. The pictures on his chest danced as he lay on his back, choking and wheezing.

Edward circled toward the car. He stopped, feet planted wide, hands open at his sides.

Yellow Cap lunged, sweeping the blade in a wide arc toward Edward's face. Edward's arm shot up and collided with the guy's wrist, stopping it in mid-flight. He locked both hands on the guy's forearm, then wrenched the guy's arm up behind his back. Yellow Cap tried twisting away, but Edward swung his leg and took him down. His head thudded against the cement.

The knife dropped. Edward picked it up. He poked the big guy with his foot, rolling him over. Yellow Cap's eyes were closed, but his chest rose and fell under his dirty T-shirt. Edward glanced at Tattoo, who was holding his throat and moaning, tucked into himself like a sow bug.

"They'll live." Edward started for the pickup. "Put the hose away, Peter. Then get the gas cap on and get in the car."

I did as I was told. Edward tested the point of the blade against his thumb, then bent and slashed the pickup's front tire. It seemed to gasp, pancaking quickly against the pavement while he sliced open a rear tire. I was in my seat, ready to roll, when he slid in and tossed the closed knife on the floor in front of me. He started the car and got us back on the highway.

"I think I set him off, Scorpio."

He grinned. "You've decided I'm your friend?"

I must have given him a blank look.

"You just called me Scorpio."

I shrugged. "You've been my friend for a while," I said. "Lila says I have a stubborn streak."

"I hadn't noticed. What'd you say to the creep?"

"I told him to get out of my face. But not until I saw you come out."

"Those guys didn't need any setting off. We weren't leaving there without trouble."

He stared out the windshield for a few minutes. "At least I forgot about being tired," he said finally.

Twenty-two

Edward was right. He'd lost that tired look back at the gas station. So he was wide awake when a siren suddenly blared out.

Red lights danced behind us. Edward eased onto the shoulder. He switched off the key, turned to me, and took a deep breath for both of us.

"I'm transporting you from Resthaven, Peter. From Resthaven to Summer Hills in Oakland. Your family's there. You were a runaway. Got it?"

I heard a door slam shut behind us, and footsteps on the pavement. "Got it."

Edward rolled down his window.

"Put both hands on the steering wheel, please," a man's voice said.

Edward placed his hands high on the wheel. The policeman—young and serious—surveyed the insides of the car. His eyes stopped for a long moment on me, and I tried to smile; I felt like crying.

"Driver's license and registration, please."

Edward handed them over.

"I hear you folks had a little trouble back at the gas stop."

Edward shifted in his seat. "A little."

"Can you tell me what happened?"

"A guy jumped Peter, here. I pulled him off, gave him a sore throat. His buddy joined in and got a headache for his trouble. Not a big deal."

The policeman looked in again. "That your knife on the floorboard?"

"It is now."

"I'll take it off your hands."

I picked up the knife and gave it to Edward. It was heavier than it looked. He passed it butt-first to the cop, who tucked it into his belt.

"What's your last name, Peter?"

I told him Larson. It was about all I could do.

"And what's your relationship to Edward, here?"

Relationship? I wasn't sure how to answer.

Edward stepped in: "Peter's been a client at the Resthaven Psychiatric Facility in Big Rock, Texas.

I'm on the staff, and I'm transporting him to the Summer Hills Facility in Oakland."

"California? Why's that?"

"His people are there. He's a runaway."

The cop positioned himself at eye level with me. "Is that true, Peter? Is Edward taking you home?"

"Yes."

"You've spent some time in the hospital where he works?"

"Yes."

"Why is that, Peter?" His eyes stayed on me.

"Depression." I tried to make my face go blank.

"Sorry," he said finally, and stood.

"You have some identification to verify your employment at the hospital, Edward?"

"Sure." Edward fished his name badge and some papers out of a pouch above the visor.

The cop studied the items one by one. "What's a mental health technician do, Edward?"

Edward told him, his voice casual and even.

"And is there a person we can contact there—a supervisor—who can verify all this?"

Edward wrote something on a scrap of paper and handed it to the cop. "Here you go," he said pleasantly. How could he be so calm?

"Wait here," the cop said, but I felt like running. He headed back to his car.

I thought about what would come next: the trip back to Resthaven, the war with my mom and Buck. What more could they do to me? Nothing, compared to what Edward might be in for. Kidnapping? Could they charge him with kidnapping?

"Sorry, Scorpio."

"My decision, Peter. Keep your chin up."

I took a breath and closed my eyes. Behind us the police radio crackled, and a woman's voice came on with a loud squawk, reciting a jumble of words and numbers. In the silence that followed I heard the cop's voice going on and on.

I tried to work out who would be on duty. What would they say? I'd run away; Edward was helping me without my parents' permission.

The tick of the engine cooling, the sighs of passing cars, the rhythm of the cop's voice marked off the minutes. Finally, the cop appeared. I tried to look natural, but I wasn't breathing.

"Your story doesn't match what the gentlemen in question told us. But we know those guys; that's not surprising. The clerk witnessed everything and verified your version. I know you're just passing through, but if you want to press charges, we could probably teach them a lesson."

Edward shook his head. "I don't think they'd learn anything."

"If you change your mind, here's my card." He gave Edward a business card. "And your things." He handed over the stuff he'd taken. "It all checks out."

"Thanks."

"Thank *you*, Mr. Lang. And I apologize for our lack of hospitality."

"No problem."

"Take it easy, son," the cop said to me, and headed back to his car.

Edward sat for a few seconds, staring straight ahead. Then we eased back onto the highway. I kept looking at him, but he wouldn't look back. He checked his mirror over and over as if he couldn't believe the cop hadn't followed us.

I couldn't believe it either. I wanted an explanation. "What happened? I was sure he was going to arrest us."

A grin crept across Edward's face. He pointed to the scrap of paper he'd given the cop. I picked it up and read the name of the person who had set us free: Sarah Gifford.

Sarah. *The cop had talked to Sarah.*

"She wanted to help," said Edward. "I told her I didn't know how, but to be ready, just in case."

I remembered her fooling me with her hurt feelings act; I remembered her grownup ways, that low, low voice. I couldn't have pulled it off; she'd probably enjoyed it.

"How did you know it would work?" I said.

"I didn't, but we didn't have a choice."

"Thank God for Sarah."

"Amen."

Edward reached in his pocket and pulled out his counter. "I don't think I want to wait, after all. Click some off for me, will you, Peter? Whatever you think that was worth."

I started clicking. I quit when my thumb got tired and Edward was way over his goal. We'd had some laughs and put a bunch more miles on the car. Two hours later we pulled off the highway and found a motel. Edward needed some sleep.

Twenty-three

We woke before dawn and got back on the road. We'd slept all afternoon and most of the night. Cars were scarce, outnumbered by trucks; towns were rare and small. Edward stuck to the speed limit, looking alert but relaxed as mile after mile slipped by.

We continued north through Utah. There was beauty in the country we passed, but we saw it on the fly with our thoughts elsewhere. We'd just crossed the border into Idaho when Edward asked a question that had been with me the whole time.

"What am I going to do with you if this turns out to be a fool's errand?"

I didn't have choices. I'd grown sick of my life with my mom and Buck. I wanted someone whose eyes would well up with love for me. I believed he was out there, remembering, waiting. But if I couldn't find him? "I'll go back."

"Home?"

"You loan me the bus fare, I'll go home. I'll put up with them until I'm old enough to leave."

"I'll *give* you the money."

"You just need to give me your address."

"I'll give you my address. So you can write me."

We went on, into Oregon. We stopped at a motel near Pendleton and managed to get in a couple games of chess. I thought maybe Edward's fatigue would fuzz up his brain. And I did survive longer than usual. But in the end the result looked way too familiar.

"Maybe next time," I said.

"You practice up against your daddy," Edward said. "Then we'll get together for a real match."

"You're on."

Early the next morning we crossed the Columbia River into Washington. I'd pictured green hills and towering mountains and blue water. Instead, the hills were low and brown; after the Columbia there was no water. I could have been in Texas, and for a moment I had a strange feeling that I was.

Two hours later the brown horizon began wearing dots of green on its shoulders. Soon the hills were higher and greener, and we were going up into the mountains, past forests and lakes, and higher to the summit of Snoqualmie Pass. I opened my window and breathed in the cool, moist air.

"Just about an hour now," Edward announced.

An hour. We started down the western side of the mountain range—a nice, gentle slope, but my stomach rose as if we'd just gone over the top on a roller coaster.

"I don't have his address," I said.

Edward pulled a piece of paper from his pocket. It was a map showing a neighborhood in a city—Seattle—with a star in the middle, and the name James Nordquist on it.

"I got the map off the Internet," said Edward. "It'll save us a little time."

"No wonder I can't beat you at chess."

"You'll have your day."

We crossed a lake on a floating bridge and reached Seattle. I tried to tell myself it looked familiar as we passed the Space Needle—Lincoln's flying saucer on stilts—but I didn't remember any of it. My doubts deepened. What was I doing? Why had I talked Edward into this?

I studied the map. "Next exit, I think."

We took the exit and headed west, then north. A lake appeared, sparkling blue, surrounded by grass, a trail, joggers, sunbathers. Its shoreline showed on the neighborhood map—Green Lake. We were only a few blocks away.

I had Edward turn right, but I was a block early, and we circled back toward the lake and found the house.

Edward parked across the street and turned off the motor. The car seemed to sigh, and then there was silence.

I stared at the house—a neat two-story, older, gray, closed-up, no sign of anyone home.

"Ready, Peter?"

I was but I wasn't. "Will you go for me?"

"Sure. But at least get out and stand by the car so he can see you."

I stood, half-leaning against the fender, while Edward crossed the street and climbed the cement steps to the yard. He looked back once before ringing the doorbell. He rang again, then glanced in the front window. I stared at the door, willing it to open, but it didn't.

"Nothing going on inside," Edward said when he got back. "Could be out for just a little while. We'll wait."

We waited in the car until the heat drove us out to the grass parking strip, where we stood, then sat. An hour passed. We walked to the lake, keeping the house in sight the whole time. My head felt like it was on a swivel.

We walked back and sat on the parking strip again, trying to look like we belonged. Although it was hot—hotter than I'd expected—I got a chill every time a car approached. But they all passed us by.

It was 3:35 when I saw the people coming from the lake. There were three of them—a woman, a little girl, and a man—walking up the sidewalk on the other side of the street. Like the man, the little girl was dark-haired and thin. Sandwiched in the middle, she held onto the man's hand, the leg of the woman's shorts.

Maybe they'd walked to the lake and now they were coming home. But to which home? We got to our feet and watched the family come closer, moving in their own little world. But they must have felt our eyes on them, following them as they approached the Nordquist house. The man, then the woman, glanced at us as if we were interesting shrubs that had just sprouted up. Then they moved on, closer to the house. Closer. And I sent them a message from my heart: *Turn; climb those steps.* I held my breath, praying for them to start up those steps.

And they did. The little girl first, Mom steadying her from behind, Dad last.

Edward moved into the street. "Mr. Nordquist?" he called out. "James Nordquist?" Edward's voice was loud above the neighborhood sounds, but friendly, and the man smiled a curious smile. I'd planned on staying by the car, but I found myself being dragged along in Edward's wake.

"Can I help you?" the man said.

The woman and little girl stopped at the front door and turned in unison. Sunlight danced off their heads as a breeze pushed up the street and coffee-brown wisps of hair blew across their faces. I looked at the man's face as I drifted closer, searching for something familiar.

"We're looking for someone." Edward stopped

in front of the man. I froze ten feet away. The man looked at me, and I wanted so badly for him to see my face and recognize a two-year-old kid under my skin. But he turned back to Edward.

"Someone I know?"

"We're looking for a man whose ex-wife would've left with their little boy about eleven years ago. We're looking for someone who hasn't seen that little boy since."

I watched the man's face. His smile faded, his eyes widened. At the edge of my vision I saw the woman and little girl start back down the walk. The man looked like he wanted to say something—his mouth closed and opened, he swallowed—but the woman beat him to it. She took his arm and stared at Edward.

"What are you saying?" she demanded.

Edward looked at me, then back at them. All eyes shifted to me.

"This young man's name is Peter," Edward told them. "Peter Nordquist, we believe. He's traveled two thousand miles—and eleven years—to find his dad."

The man spoke, a bare whisper: "Peter?" He

moved down the walk, down the steps, the woman and little girl in tow. I wanted to go to him, but I felt light-headed, afraid that one step would drop me to my knees.

"Peter?" he said again, louder, but he shook his head as if he only half-believed the idea, that it was too much. Then he was standing right in front of me, letting his wary eyes wander over my face while I studied his.

Suddenly I knew. I knew it as he raised his hand and touched my cheek and pushed his fingers through my hair until his hand rested on the back of my head and he was staring into my eyes, his eyes filling with tears.

He pulled me close, pressing my head against his chest, wrapping me up in such a powerful hug I could barely breathe, but I didn't want him to stop. "Peter!" he said, loud now, between sobs.

I felt his weight, but I couldn't hold him up, he couldn't hold me up. We collapsed in slow motion to the grass. "Peter!" he shouted, helping me back to my feet. "Laura! Missie! It's Peter! It's our boy!"

The woman and little girl came closer.

"How—?" the woman began. She looked at me,

then at the man, then back at me again. The little girl kept her eyes on me. Suddenly the woman smiled, a big wondrous smile. "It *is* Peter!" she said. She began crying as she hugged me, then the man, then both of us together.

I caught a glimpse of Edward's smiling face, blurry through my tears, then felt a tug on the leg of my shorts. I looked down at the little girl as she stared up at me.

"Peter," she said, "you've *grown!*"

I laughed. We all laughed. Then for just a thin second I felt a cold twinge of doubt. Was it all a dream? It seemed like a dream. But I looked at the faces, felt the arms, heard the voices, smelled the sweet summer air, and I knew it was real. Wide awake, I was having a real dream. And I wanted it to go on forever.

Letters

Dear Sarah,

I was going to call you, but the counselor I've been seeing told me I should try writing things down. I decided to take her advice.

You probably know most of the story from Lila by now. You wouldn't believe how much Scorpio did for me.

The end of the story is that I'm really with my dad. But maybe I wouldn't have ever gotten here if you hadn't talked to Scorpio, and distracted the tech, and fooled the cop. Thank you, thank you, thank you!

For the past eleven years my dad's been searching everywhere for me. He really was a fisherman when my mom took me. He was

fishing in Alaska when we left. He stopped
fishing and started looking. He got a job as
a flight attendant (Lincoln's man with wings)
so he could afford to travel to a lot of places.
He talked to the police and newspapers and
TV and passed out my picture wherever he
went.

He got to Texas, but never close to
Deadwood. Even though he kept running into
dead ends, he kept looking. He started writing
articles for travel magazines so he could get to
even more places. He met Laura, who's an
airline pilot, and she helped him look. No luck
finding me, but they got married and had a
little girl. Now I have a sister named Missie.

My dad won't admit it, but I think he'd given
up hope of seeing me again. I think he was just
going through the motions. I catch him staring at
me sometimes when he thinks I'm not paying
attention, and he has tears in his eyes. He says
he's just happy, but I wonder. We've got each
other now, and he won't let me out of his sight.
He's like a shadow, but I don't ever want to lose
him.

One thing I didn't think about was relatives, but I have relatives here, too. My dad's mom and dad are close by, and my mom's mom. I have *grandparents!* I have an aunt and uncle and cousins. None of them ever heard from my mom once we left. Maybe that was why she seemed sad so much of the time.

I miss her, more than I thought I would, but not so much that I want to see her again very soon. I know she was probably sick when she took me, and maybe she still is, but I'm having a hard time forgiving her for what she did. I miss Lincoln a ton, but I've talked to him on the phone a lot. My mom's been okay with it. She's even talking about letting him come up here. I think she knows my dad has her backed into a corner. So far no one's decided what to do about the kidnapping charges against her.

I miss you, too. I don't miss Buck. Tell Eugene hi. Write me back.
Love,
Peter

❄

Dear Peter,

Thank you for writing to me. The phone call with the cop was scary but exciting and fun, especially after I heard you made it all the way to Seattle and really found your dad. I'm going to have a story to tell my kids, but they probably won't believe it.

It's not the same around here without you, so I'm fixing to check out. I've gained three pounds since you left. I'm feeling fat, but they tell me it will take five *more* pounds and an attitude adjustment to get me home. I can fake the attitude adjustment, but putting on five more pounds makes me nervous. Cat says I'd put on weight faster if I quit smoking. I think I'll keep smoking. But I *am* ready to get out of here.

Pretty soon I'll be the only one left. John has decided to give up on the Eugene stuff (or it decided to give up on him). We're having real conversations now. And they're telling him he'll be able to go home soon.

I'm seeing a new shrink, and she's cool. I told her she'd be cooler if she took up smoking, but she's a runner. She says *I'd* make a good runner.

What do you think?

I saw Lincoln on TV again tonight. He's a cutie. Send me a picture of your dad, and do it quick. I might not be here much longer.
Love,
Sarah

❉

Dear Peter,

The rumors were flying, so I finally got up the nerve to ask your mom if they were true. She didn't bite my head off or anything, but she didn't act like she wanted to talk much about it. She said you'd found out where your dad was living and left the hospital to be with him. She gave me your address. I didn't ask my biggest questions, which were why she had you believing he was dead, and how you found out he wasn't. Write back and tell me what really happened.

Things are going okay with me. Football turnouts have started, and my butt is definitely dragging in this heat. School starts soon. I expect it won't be the same without you. It's already not the same around here. It's been real quiet, but I don't think that will last.

A reporter came to our house yesterday, asking questions about you. We didn't have much to tell her, but she looked to be hot on the trail of a story.

Once it hits the newspaper, and the TV folks get ahold of it, I think things will get real lively in Deadwood.

I hope you're doing great. Write soon.
Your bud,
Dillon

※

Hi Peter,

I hope you or your folks are checking your e-mail, because there's a note from me. I promised to let you know how I was doing once I got down here. The answer is, great! My job is good, I've got a nice place to stay, and I like the city and its people. One, especially. Sister Moses (Arabella) and I have hit it off like we've known each other forever. She says she loves what I've done with my life. I tell her it's mostly her doing.

And yours. I believe you had a hand in where
I ended up. I'm never going to forget your
reunion with your daddy. It's in my mind like a
movie, and I play it back every day. Write and tell
me what's going on with you. You best be
working on your chess for our rematch.
Your traveling partner,
Scorpio

*

Dear Peter,

Mom is helping me with this letter, but I
wrote your name myself. Do you think the P
looks like a mailbox? I do, but Mom says it's
a pretty good P, especially for someone just
getting ready to start kindergarten.

Thank you for calling me yesterday. You
sounded really close. I wish you were close,
because I miss you. Mom says I'll get to see
you before too long, though—probably at
Thanksgiving or Christmastime. She says the
grownups are working on it. But I looked at
my calendar, and Thanksgiving is far away.
Christmas is real far.

Mom says I should mark off the days, so
I am. I'm using my dinosaur stickers. So far
I've stuck on a T-Rex and an Apatosaurus.

Sarah called me. She says she isn't as skinny
now. She's nice. I think she likes you.

Last night I had a dream. You and the
man with wings were paddling a canoe across
a lake. The sun was going down. It was low in
the sky, but I could see the sunshine on your face.
You were smiling.
Love,
Lincoln

P.S. I wrote my name, too.